Jon Bragg Giant Problem

Jon Bragg, Volume 3

Kenney Myers

*Thank you for believing,
in the power of words!*

Kenney Myers

Published by Kenney Myers, 2024.

JON BRAGG GIANT PROBLEM

First edition. July 11, 2024.

ISBN: 978-1736571194

Written by Kenney Myers.

Table of Contents

In loving memory of Joe Clapp and Don Myers. Two benevolent giants that inspired me and shaped this story and my life in different ways. You are sorely missed and never forgotten.

As you read this please take a moment to think about the giants that have shaped your own life and helped make you who you are today.

Summer Ends

Jon

I FORCE OPEN MY EYES as the sun floods its way through my blinds, urging—no, imploring—me to wake up. It's the last day of summer vacation after all, and there is much to do.

I actually love school so, for me, I have more of a feeling of excitement about tomorrow than anything else. I cannot wait to tear into the next book for AP English and to discuss the meaning of every noun, verb, and adjective with Mr. Young. He is easily my favorite teacher, but mostly because I love reading and writing so much. In fact, I hope to have a discussion with him about some of the books I have read over the last few weeks.

I have had quite a bit of time to read since the incident at scout camp. For me, that has meant reading everything I can about the afterlife according to Norse myths.

Hmm ... myths. That reminds me about the last book I read that described how in ancient society, myths had a different meaning than they do today. Back then, myths meant something more like stories handed down that were more fact than fiction. They needed to be passed on from generation to generation somehow so they would not be forgotten. Nowadays, a myth is assumed to be something made up. It's funny how people jump to conclusions based upon their own experiences and beliefs. As I have learned over the last year, it's not always so clear cut. I am definitely more careful about how I interpret what I read now, that's for sure.

1

I reach over to my nightstand to feel for my phone. I could look, but I know it's there somewhere. I blindly unplug the charging cable and plop the phone right in front of my face. You see, I am one of those guys who likes to read close. Almost so close that the phone touches my nose. I don't know why I do that, but I suspect it goes back to when I was younger and first reading. Some habits are hard to break. It's something that Jill loves to make fun of me for, but hey, if that's the best my sis can come up with to tease me, I'll take it. I often have my "nose buried in a book" everywhere I go, so it's a running joke at this point. It's not really funny, but lots of people seem to think it is, so I guess I am glad I bring them so much joy.

My mind drifts back to my phone. I am a creature of habit, if there ever was one, so I have my home screen set up a specific way and work from left to right across the top. I check my email first, then Instagram, then Facebook, and finally Snapchat. I have considered switching the order since Darla likes using Snapchat so much, but again, I am just resistant to change, so I leave it be.

I decided that since I have no particular place I need to be today, to go ahead and scroll through the messages that I have saved between Darla and me. Our experience at camp was so intense, and I'm shocked by how much she remembers. I cannot figure out how she was able to remember everything after the Asgardian Protection Society (APS) nurse used her powers to wipe the memory of everyone at the camp. I keep trying to ask her about it, but she changes the subject almost as quickly as I bring it up. I guess I don't blame her. It's a lot to take in, and I can respect that.

It took me quite a while to accept what I was—I mean, am. Being a descendant of an Asgardian god doesn't come up often in casual conversation and, until last year, I would have told you it was completely impossible. Now, I live the impossible, so my position on the matter has changed. I'm just thankful that I am a descendant of

Bragi, the god of poetry, versus being a descendant of Loki or one of the gods with a darker reputation.

The APS classifies me as "a" Bragi. I guess there could be more of his descendants like me out there. I know Grandpa used to be one before he lost his powers when Coach Locke killed Grandma and extracted his blue essence.

After having two run-ins with Coach Locke and his son, Dustin, two Lokis, and narrowly defeating them twice, I would be quite happy to never meet another descendant of Loki again. They are quite the stubborn lot, to say the least, and so vindictive and bent on revenge. That is why I am reading up on the afterlife. I just want to make sure there is no loophole that is going to allow them to come back into my life and threaten someone close to me again. First, they took Marc, and then they took Darla, whom I wasn't really even that close to, at least not yet.

I feel the anger building up inside of me just thinking about what they would have done to them if I didn't stop Loki first with the blood spell, and then second by using the troll cross to send them straight to Hades. Of course, I would feel better if Hades wasn't actually run by a child of Loki's, but I am positive nobody would be foolish enough to bargain with them and let them pass to another realm. Certainly not all the way back to this realm. No god or giant would be that stupid, right?

I shudder at the thought.

I also keep thinking about the APS finding giant DNA throughout the camp as they were cleaning up the mess that we—well, mostly me—made. They are convinced that someone else at the camp comes from a line of giants. However, we have not been able to identify who it could be.

Grandpa says that giants typically have similar gifts compared to gods. They are typically highly attractive on the outside but could be either good or bad on the inside. It just depends on the path they have chosen to pursue, which is honestly the same for all of us. In any event, as I remember, they also have the same possible characteristics as Asgardians. They could be strong, smart, or skilled in some particular thing, which basically describes almost everyone who was at the scout camp. We had some brilliant computer geeks, like Josh and Aiden; some incredible jocks, like Sam and Taylor; musicians, skilled outdoorsmen, and on and on. Most importantly, nobody stood out as being particularly evil in any way. Other than the draugr that was formerly Coach Locke and his similar son, of course.

I am really hoping that the APS got it wrong, and it was Coach Locke's DNA that was somehow found and misidentified as being from a different giant line. After all, they were actually dead and in spirit form (draugr) so that has to mess with one's DNA, right? Does a ghost even have DNA?

Grandpa did take me to the APS coroner's lab where the victims were being held. One of the powers that I have been gifted with is the ability to look into any animals' eyes and see what happened to them as they met their demise. It's a bit like a dream that is locked into their short-term memory that hasn't been fully erased. When I recite a rhyme that includes the color of their eyes, presumed death, or their current state, it triggers the memory to surface and play for me in my mind.

When I used this power on the man that freed Coach Locke from his troll cross burial, I only saw Coach Locke, who made quick work of him. So, unfortunately, that lead was kind of a dead end. Oh boy, "dead end"—I am my father's son. That's not punny—it really isn't—but I have no doubt that some would find it to be. To me, it's just depressing because I was hoping to be able to uncover any other giant who may have been present.

I did see something interesting in the eyes of a buck that the APS found at the camp. What I saw from him was either a nightmare or a giant wolf that had mercilessly hunted him down and killed him. The strange thing was the eyes of this wolf, which were highly unusual, and I couldn't really adequately describe them to Grandpa. While it was an unusually massive wolf, it seemed possible for the woods surrounding Harmony Grove.

Grandpa, Marc, and I constantly remain on high alert. We will be doing our best to focus our attention on the students from Grinwell and Bluehill who were at our camp this summer. Right now, the top of the list is Sam. Sam is Darla's friend, but he is enormous and beasted his way through just about every competition at the camp. I was mostly holding back and doing my best to avoid using any magic or to show any abnormal skills. I also get just a bit flustered around girls that I like, which brings me back to focusing on Darla.

She seems to have forgiven me for getting her into danger and/ or believes that it wasn't my fault. It kind of was, but mostly, it was just Coach Locke trying to make me suffer by hurting someone I care for. I really do care for her, and I cannot wait to see her in person. Unfortunately, she has been grounded since we got back from camp, so that is why we only communicate right now through Snapchat. That's also only possible whenever her dad lets her have her phone when her mother is away or not with them.

Her dad sure seems like a standup guy. Her mother, on the other hand, is just not nice to her at all. I'm so glad my mom is not like that. I sure am fortunate to have been born into the Bragg family, for many reasons.

Cousin Chat

Darla

IT'S BEEN A LONG LAST part of the summer break with my mother pushing me every way possible. I am doing more chores than ever now as part of my punishment that never ends. I spend the day in the fields with Dad, which is easily the best part of my day. Mostly, because Dad snags my phone for me and, during our lunch breaks, he lets me have a few moments of normalcy while we eat in the field, the barn, or wherever we happen to be working that day. He always says, "Darlin', I know how hard this is for you, but your mother is only doing what she thinks is best for the family." I just shake my head most days when this reminder is offered up. I am not trying to be rude to Dad, I just cannot fathom why all of this is necessary for what they believe is me getting lost at scout camp.

If they knew what really happened, they might go easier on me. I am so tempted to tell at least him. Surely, he would understand if I explained that I was kidnapped by a ghost, hauled underground, and held captive until a descendant of a Norse god came and saved me. Yeah, on second thought, I'll just eat my lunch and continue scrolling Snapchat, taking fish-face selfies, rolling my eyes, and sending them to Jenny, Jess, and even Jon.

I know it's his fault that I was kidnapped in the first place—sort of—but he did save me in the end. Of course, he did that only after making the situation ten times worse in typical Jon Bragg style. He is the most interesting mixture of a hot mess and a true hero that I have ever known. I wish I could tell Dad all about him, too, but I'm sure that if I mentioned any of this, I would get a visit from that team of people they sent to wipe out Jenny's and everyone else's memory who was at camp. I don't want that to happen to my family. Well, at least not to Dad. Mother, on the other hand, maybe.

Since my eight "cousins" arrived to stay with us, my whole world has been turned upside down. Mother refers to them as cousins but, to be honest, they are from all over the world. And, as far as I can tell, they are distant relatives, at best. That said, Mother insists, so I will introduce them as cousins to appease her. I have been using Snapchat to describe this gaggle of girls to Jess and Jenny. Even Jon. Although Jon keeps asking me questions about camp this summer, as if I want to relive those memories. For being such a "powerful" person, he sure can be dense. Why would I want to think about that every day? I quickly changed the subject by talking about work on the farm, work at the house, and the small amount of free time in-between.

After I get done in the field with Dad, Mother always has a long list of chores for me to work on. Usually, I am doing laundry for the whole house because the other girls are "our guests." If I hear her say that one more time, I am going to scream.

You know what this is like? It's like I am Cinderella but instead of her being the wicked stepmother, she is *my* real mother; and instead of me being the daughter who gets pampered, I am the one who is slaving away while the other eight girls spend time with Mother doing who knows what for hours at a time. Mother just barks out orders at me and runs off with the other girls, saying, "Be sure to have everything done before we get back, and then off to bed with you!"

I have half a mind to just mess up every chore so that she decides I am "worthless" and need to be taught a "lesson" by making me stay in my room alone. Honestly, it would be better than doing these chores. Maybe I could make friends with the field mice that we are always catching in the closets. Ha! Wouldn't that be fitting. Just like Cinderella.

If I am really lucky, I'll meet my fairy godmother, go to the dance, lose my slipper, and be saved by my prince. Nah, I'd rather just grin and bear it and not let her have the pleasure of knowing she broke me. *You know what? Bring it, Mother. I can handle whatever you decide to throw at me.*

As for the actual stepsisters/cousins, they are a bunch of cackling suck-ups who hang on Mother's every word. I'm sure she thinks that is awesome. Finally, some real girls who want to do girlie things instead of Boy Scouts, sports, and hard labor, like me. Whatever. They can have her.

As far as my cousins go, they are quite the lot. I try to avoid them as much as possible, but seeing as I don't have my phone in the house, the best I can do is describe them to Jenny, Jess, and even Jon. It's just easier if I snap the same stuff since I have such a short amount of time with my phone every day.

Over the past week and a half, I decided to take turns describing one of them every day. I opt to start with the worst and work my way to the least offensive.

Gadara, or "Gaddy," is a red-headed girl who is always in a bad mood. Big shock, right? She is a walking, fiery-red stereotype. She is short but stout, the kind of girl who should be on the bottom of the cheerleading pyramid, or in dance, catching the girl leaping but would never accept that lowly status. Instead, she makes the other girls try to catch her heavy butt then yells at them when they fail. Don't get me wrong—she isn't fat; she is just all muscle. She has a long nose to match her long face, but at the same time is exotic and oddly pretty, I guess.

She could easily be my mother's daughter with the way she acts like the queen bee. Literally, the only person in the house she doesn't dare boss around is my mother. The other girls and I are obviously fair game. Needless to say, she is my least favorite cousin, and I'm pretty sure she knows exactly how I feel about her.

I'd like to knock her down a few pegs, to say the least. Someday, she will get what is coming to her. I'm sure the consequences will be severe, but that sure would be glorious to see.

Ronda, or "Ronny," is honestly stunning. She could possibly give Jess a run for her money at school this year. Unlike Jess though, she has dark brown hair with blonde tips that hang just below her shoulders, as if they are pointing down to her model-like body. Seriously, without a doubt, she is going to be the most popular girl on the farm with the Bluehill and Grinwell boys.

However, her fatal flaw, in my book, is she is an emotional, needy, hot mess. She is the biggest drama queen I have ever met. Everything is so exaggerated with her that I almost like her less than Gaddy. Almost, but Gaddy is a stone-cold b—no capital B. Ronny, though, seems to make everyone in the room either incredibly happy or incredibly sad, depending on how she feels at the moment. Except me, of course, because I couldn't care less. I barely know these girls, and they don't even give me a second thought, so why should I worry about how Ronny is feeling? Whatever.

I hate school, but it is going to be a welcome reprieve from home. It's going to be so weird between going to Grinwell versus Bluehill, plus having what is the equivalent of eight instant sisters hanging around. Hopefully, I can ditch them quickly and just spend time with Jenny, Jess, and Jon, and just forget about those jerks at least for a few hours.

I wonder what this year will hold. Am I going to get the chance to join the wrestling team? I cannot help but daydream about showing those boys how strong us girls can be. I am definitely not going to back down, and I am never going to give up. I am a Towns, and we don't give up. We keep going until time runs out. Determined to not get pinned down and resolute on putting up a good fight.

That's going to be me this year. No more dance and cheer for me. I'm a wrestler now.

First Day

Jon

THE FIRST DAY OF SCHOOL is always exciting for me, but this one is different. I must have changed clothes eight times, trying to get something that I was comfortable wearing. I know this is all about Darla because, normally, I just grab a shirt, take a whiff, and slide it on. If this is going to be a regular thing for me, I am going to need to allocate more time to getting around and set my alarm for a bit earlier.

Let's not go crazy, though; it's just the first day.

Speaking of Darla, I might as well take a quick snap. We do have a thirty-six-day streak going, and I might as well let her know what to look for this morning when she gets to school. I'll be available to show her around if she needs it, even though I'm sure Jess will snatch up that honor. Jess and her are already close because they are a part of the same dance company, which happens to be the one where my sister goes to …

Knock. Knock. Knock.

Speaking of the devil …

"C'mon, loser!" Jill screeches through the door. "You look pretty enough, and Mom made us breakfast. So, let's go!"

I just close my eyes, take a breath, and yell back, "Coming." I really didn't have any desire to get into it with Jill this morning. I'm sure she is excited to be starting high school. That is going to be different. We haven't been at the same school in a couple of years. I don't mind, though; it certainly is going to take less time.

Ever since I got my driver's license, I had to drop her off and pick her up from her school. Now, she can just go along for the ride with Marc and me. Much simpler, much better.

As I get down the stairs, I see that Mom has outdone herself this year. We have a full-on breakfast buffet laid out for us. That's great because I am starving.

I put a mound of food on my plate, and Mom says, "Slow down, Jonboy. Be sure to leave some for your dad—he hasn't eaten yet."

I look over to apologize, but before I get the words out, Mom says, "It's okay. I have more pancakes coming. I just wanted to let you know Dad hasn't had any yet. Eat up."

Whew. That's a relief.

I start shoveling in the food as quickly as possible, which merits Mom saying, "Don't forget to breathe, Jon. It's not a race."

Jill thinks this is hilarious and continues glaring at me as if she has been waiting for me to finish for hours. I'm sorry, but Mom went through all of this trouble, so I am going to have some of everything.

We have oatmeal with peanut butter in it, which I love, scrambled eggs with shredded cheese, pancakes, toast, and chocolate milk to wash it all down. A fine breakfast, indeed, and an amazing start to the day. That reminds me ...

"Thanks for breakfast, Mom."

"My pleasure, Jonboy."

I realize that somewhere between oatmeal and pancakes, Dad made his way to the table. He has coffee and is intently looking at his phone, scrolling through messages and whatever else Dad looks at every morning.

Without looking up, he asks, "What are you most looking forward to this year in school?"

I want to tell him it's too early in the day for questions like this, but I tell him, "I am looking forward to AP English. I have some books I want to discuss with Mr. Young."

"Book nerd," Jill quips.

"Jill, be nice," Dad admonishes. "Jon, I think that sounds wonderful. I'm sure Mr. Young will enjoy that, as well. What time do you have to be there this morning?"

That causes instant panic to come over me as I look at my phone to check the time, and then I sigh in relief. "Oh, we have about thirty minutes, so plenty of time. But Marc and I wanted to get there early to greet some of our friends from Bluehill."

Jill mocks, "Like who, Jon? Darrrrrrrla?" She draws out the R's for dramatic effect.

"As a matter of fact, yes. Darla, Sam, Taylor, and some of the others we met at scout camp."

To which, Jill responds, "Scout nerd."

Dad just shakes his head and chuckles. "Sound like a good plan, Jon."

With that, we clear the dishes, wipe off the table, and then start gathering up our bookbags to head out the door.

We just about get to the front door when Mom says, "Pictures." She comes flying from the kitchen at full speed, and that stops Jill and I dead in our tracks.

I look at Jill, and she rolls her eyes back at me. Her displeasure makes me smile.

"Of course," I say to Mom. "Where would you like us?" That's totally unnecessary because, every year, we take a picture by the front door.

Mom takes my picture then Jill's. Finally, she takes one of both of us.

"Get closer. Like you like each other, please."

I put my arm behind Jill's back, not actually touching her, but good enough to look like it on camera. This pleases Mom, who ends our photo shoot.

Seeing Jill is relieved, I decide to ask Mom, "Do you think Dad wants any pictures with us, too?"

Jill gives me the death glare as Mom says, "That's a good idea, Jon."

As Mom goes to get Dad and Jill punches me on the shoulder, I literally laugh out loud. Yep, this is going to be a fun year of messing with Jill. Definitely looking forward to that.

Dad is about as thrilled as Jill to be in the pictures, but it's all over quick enough. Mom and Dad then give each of us a hug and we stroll over to the Corolla.

Jill goes to get in the front seat, and I ask, "What do you think you are doing?"

She looks at me defiantly and says, "Look, Jon, I am not going to sit in the back every morning. You are *my* brother, and this is *our* car."

Hold up. Nope, this is not going to happen.

"This is *my* car, and you know good and well that Marc rides shotgun. That is how it has always been and how it will always be."

Jill responds, "Well, I am sitting up here until we pick him up then."

Okay, sure.

I look at her really quickly and just say:

> "Jill, it's really quite clear,
> When Marc gets in, you'll switch to the rear.
> No need for complaints or anything to fear,
> Just move to the back when he gets here."

She rolls her eyes at me. "You are so weird." With that, she plops into the front seat with a defiant and victorious grin on her face, and then she proceeds to adjust the seat. Forward and back, forward and back, back a little more, forward a little more.

This goes on for at least thirty seconds before she finally stops long enough for me to ask, "Are you comfortable?"

She looks me straight in the eyes and says, "Quite, thank you. No, thank you."

I surrender and sigh. "Just buckle up so we can get going."

She clicks in and replies with a mock salute, "Sir, yes, sir."

As we pull up to Marc's house, he comes running out his front door as if he couldn't possibly be more excited. Of course, I also know he has been using his cell phone to track where we are. Since he rides with us so often, we long ago added him to our Life360 app, which lets us track each other (Mom, Dad, Grandpa, Jill, Marc, and I).

As he nears the car, he sees Jill is in the front seat, and that causes him to stop dead in his tracks, look at me, and shrug.

Without me needing to say a word, Jill gets out of the car and hops into the back seat as if that was her plan all along.

Marc flashes a smile, plops his bag on the floor of the Corolla, and jumps into his seat. "Good morning, hero."

I shoot him a dirty look, and he recovers by saying, "Coming to save the day by giving me a ride to school. Thanks, buddy."

I just shake my head as Jill mocks, "Jon, you are *my* hero, too."

I moan, "Yeah, yeah, yeah. Enough, you two."

Traffic Jam

Darla

AFTER RUSHING THROUGH my chores this morning as quickly as possible, I'm trying to get ready for the first day of school, juggling texts from Jess and Jenny to see how their morning is going. I'm really glad to have my phone back on a regular basis. Or, as Dad told Mother, I need my phone in "case of an emergency." *Thank you, Dad, it worked.*

I'd be completely lost without Dad and in a total state of depression. He is my ray of sunshine in the midst of a never-ending thunderstorm. My beacon of light that guides me back into a happy place, like a boat lost at sea that catches a glimpse of a lighthouse and sets its course straight toward the light.

Ugh, no time for dramatic thoughts like that right now. I'm literally the last into the bathroom behind our "guests."

To complicate matters, Jenny is sending snaps of outfits at a record pace. She had a plan going into the morning, but as soon as she put on her day one outfit, she decided it made her look too "hippy." Of course, I reassure her that no matter what she wears she is probably never going to be happy. I wish she could see herself like I see her. She is a strong, confident girl who is an amazing friend—nothing else really matters.

That's a bit heavy of a conversation to have as we rush around, though, so I just tell her to go with her first plan and that it is "stunning". She replies with a heart emoji, and we are out of that

16

situation mostly unscathed. If only everything this morning were that easy.

I swear these girls are animals. They have left the bathroom totally destroyed. There are towels hanging on the shower, the towel bar, every hook on the back of the door, and a couple even on the floor. To make matters worse, they seem to have taken every drop of shampoo, conditioner, and even soap. Wonderful, just wonderful.

I dig around in my room for some of the travel-sized beauty products that I took to camp with me and, thankfully, there is just enough left in them.

I run through the shower as fast as humanly possible and just decide to run a brush through my hair a few times. Then I stare at the mirror for a second. That's going to have to do for today. Thank goodness I don't wear makeup because there is no time for that nonsense today. I'm sure the other girls are all glammed up, which is going to make me like them even less, but what else is new?

Normally, I wouldn't care at all about how I look before school because it's school. This morning, though, I do have a bit of an uneasy feeling or, as Mother would say, "butterflies." I just haven't seen *him* in a while. I wonder how he is going to react to me. Is he going to be excited to see me? Is it going to be weird? What am I saying, of course it will be weird. It's Jon—every situation is awkward when Jon is involved. Who knows? I might not even see him. It's a much bigger school, and I have no idea where he might be, where his locker is located, or even what classes he is taking.

Speaking of Jon, I had another nightmare about him last night … For some reason, it always ends up the same. Jon is in trouble, and I have to figure out some way to save him. Last night, he was locked up in a cage or something like that. It was a weird, jail-like scenario, and something was attacking him. It's so crazy because, in reality, it was the other way around—Jon saved me. All I know is that these dreams are really getting old, and I just wish there was someone—anyone—who I could talk to about them. If I tried, though, I'm sure it would just lead to some sort of counseling sessions or worse—conversations with Mother about me needing to stop being a "silly, petulant baby all the time."

Speaking of my drill sergeant.

CLAP! CLAP! CLAP!

This sounds comes thundering up the stairs, and that can only mean one thing.

Mother is ready to go.

Perfect, I am running late on the first day, thanks to these stupid girls. I'm so sick of them already.

I run down the stairs, through the kitchen, grab a banana and some lunch money, and then run out the front door. Normally, Mother would be waiting by the door, tapping her foot, but this time, she's already in the Tahoe. And to add to my annoyance, she taps on the horn a few times and, with her thumb out, makes a gesture to tell me to get into the back. She actually doesn't say anything, but I know what it means because the back is open and every seat in the Tahoe is occupied by one of our "guests."

The Tahoe only really fits nine if we squeeze in tight, but since Mother has decided she needs to go to school to make sure the cousins don't "need her on the first day," there is no seat left for me.

I barely crawl into the back when Mother presses the button to close the automatic door. I mumble under my breath, "I'm in, Mother. No problem, but thanks for checking." I literally whisper it, but when I look up, I see her death glare coming back at me in the mirror.

Her look is always intense, but I know she somehow heard me, and this is her way of telling me not to push it. Fine. I'm literally scrunched into the back in a space that is only really meant to hold a few bags of groceries. This is a perfect representation of what my life is like now—thrown in the back like a sack of potatoes while the other girls enjoy the luxury of an actual seat. Is it really too much to ask to have a seat? I think not.

Olga turns around and says, "Good morning, Darla. You barely made it."

I roll my eyes and just think to myself, *State the obvious much?*

She continues on, "I'm so excited about school, aren't you? I can't wait to meet all of the other kids and see what they are like. It's going to be the best."

Ugh. Sugary sweetness, it is way too early in the morning for this, so I just close my eyes and pretend like none of them are there. How wonderful would that be? If they weren't there, I would be driving myself to school and picking up Jenny. That would be so much better. In fact, it brings a smile to my face.

Olga grins. "There it is. Finally, a smile. I knew you had it in you."

Right, you keep thinking that Olga.

I do my best contortionist impression to take off my backpack so I can try to get at least slightly less uncomfortable.

Just when I am almost over it, Mother speaks up, and the chatter from within the Tahoe dies down. I realize that she must have said something directed at me because all heads are turned in my direction and Mother is looking at me in the mirror.

"What?" I ask.

Mother aggressively repeats loudly, "Darla, after school today, you *will* be joining the rest of us in our training sessions. We have been patient enough with you, but now I must insist you do your part."

I mumble, "Sure, my part, whatever." Well, that was an unpopular response, to say the least.

"*Darla Bara Towns*, you will *not* disrespect me in front of your cousins. You *will* be there. Full stop, got it?"

I relent, "Yes, Mother, I understand." I fake another smile and take some comfort as the heads turn forward and go down. Surely, even these cold-hearted B's have to feel a little sorry for me, as if I care. They can all suck eggs. I'm over all of this already.

Olga turns around as if she is about to talk, and I just put my hand up and shake my head. "Not now. I need a minute."

Early Birds

Jon

AS I DRIVE THROUGH Grinwell, I keep seeing things that remind me of the summer. We drive past several yards that Marc and I took care of, and still will until later in the fall. We really need to think about a better way to run our lawncare business for next year. We may even decide to expand and recruit some more people from school. That won't be easy, but maybe some of the new kids from Bluehill will be interested. They seemed pretty cool at camp.

We drive by Mr. Lemke's house and notice him on the front porch, waving at all of us kids as we drive by. He has two of his cats on his lap, and the rest are engulfing the porch around him. Boy, does he love cats. I have a much deeper appreciation for Mr. Lemke now, and if anyone ever says something negative about him, I am definitely going to defend his honor. He's a great man and just happens to love animals. There is absolutely nothing wrong with that.

I make the final turn up the hill that leads to the school parking lot, at least where our class gets to park, and the car bounces slightly on the uneven asphalt as we jump into our dirt/rock parking lot. Beside me, Marc is still fiddling with the radio, trying to find a decent station at the last second that isn't blasting commercials. It's hard to sound cool pulling up to school, jamming to a radio ad for Alka Selzer. Jill is sunk into the back seat, tapping away on her phone with a level of focus usually reserved for brain surgery. I'm pretty sure she's trying not to be seen with us, but it doesn't really bother me. She's quiet, and that is quite fine by me.

As I pull around to our designated parking area, my heart sinks a little. The only parking spot left is sandwiched between Brad's Camaro and a monster truck that seems to belong to another member of the football team because the number seventy-eight is taped on the back window of the truck. I can't believe so many people showed up early today, but I guess with Bluehill and Grinwell merging, everyone wanted to be sure to get a parking spot.

"Great, just great," I mutter as I maneuver the Corolla into the tight space. That is definitely one advantage to this car—it makes finding a parking spot a lot easier.

Marc glances over and smirks. "Better hope you don't need to get out in a hurry."

"Thanks for the vote of confidence," I reply dryly, turning off the engine and looking in the rearview mirror at Jill. "Hello? We are here."

Jill barely looks up from her phone. "Duh, nerd. I see my friends. Later, losers."

Before I can say anything, like where to meet after school, Jill has jumped out of the car, smacking the truck next to us with her door, and is running toward a group of girls who are already shrieking with delight. As soon as she gets to them, they jump up and down, screaming even louder, which I didn't know was possible.

Marc and I exchange a glance, both wincing at the noise.

"Why do girls always have to scream when they see each other?" Marc asks, shaking his head.

"Beats me?" I tell him, grabbing my backpack. "Come on; let's go."

As soon as we carefully slide out of our doors, we go in the opposite direction of the screaming because that is just going to continue as more of Jill's friends show up. I decide to let her have her moment although, secretly, I think for a minute about running over, jumping up and down, and mocking her. Nah, that wouldn't be cool.

As we walk toward the school, I notice Marc glancing at me out of the corner of his eye.

"What?" I ask.

"So, who do you want to be with now? Jess or Darla?" he asks, a knowing grin spreading across his face.

I sigh. "Not this again. Can we just focus on getting through the first day of school?"

"I'm serious, Jon. You had a thing at scout camp with Darla, but Jess wasn't there. Who knows how you are going to feel when you see her? It might be awkward. You know, a superhero needs to have his girl figured out. Superman had Lois Lane, Spiderman had Mary Jane Watson, and the big question is: who is it for you?"

I just shake my head and brush all this off. "For the last time, I am not a superhero. Let's just drop it, okay?"

Marc shrugs. "Fine, fine. But you are going to have to figure it out soon."

Before I can respond, we reach the entrance of the school. And, just as I am about to step inside, I almost bump straight into Mr. Young.

"Ah, Jon. Just the person I wanted to see," Mr. Young says, his eyes lighting up behind his thick glasses. "How was your summer? Did you get through the reading list?"

I force a smile. "It was good, Mr. Young, and I read everything on the list twice."

"Excellent, excellent. What are you reading now?" Mr. Young asks, genuinely interested.

I shift my weight from one foot to the other, knowing this conversation could take a while. Honestly, I am reading about my heritage, but I can't really talk with Mr. Young about giants and Asgard. At least, not in five minutes. So, I decide to go with something from the reading list. "I'm reading *To Kill a Mockingbird* again. I think I appreciate it more every time I read it."

Mr. Young nods enthusiastically. "Ah, a classic. Harper Lee's work is timeless. What do you think of the themes of racial injustice and moral growth?"

I launch into a thoughtful response, but my mind is partly on the clock. I can see Marc out of the corner of my eye, slowly edging away and eventually wandering off. There is no way to answer a question like that quickly.

Mr. Young must have caught it, too, but a little too late.

"Marc, I think you are going to like what we are reading in class first this year. Marc?"

Marc is already turning the corner in the hall toward our lockers.

"Well, it's a Norse classic. Is Marc still into Thor?"

I reply, "Yeah, you could say that. I am actually really interested in it, as well, Mr. Young. I'm looking forward to class today. See you in a bit."

By the time I manage to extricate myself from the conversation with Mr. Young, the halls are beginning to fill up. I take a deep breath and start walking, only to run into Brad, who is lounging against the lockers with what looks like half the football team.

"Hey, Jonboy," Brad calls out, a smirk playing on his lips. "How was scout camp? What did you do this time to make them shut it down early?"

I feel my face flush. "Nothing, Brad. I didn't do anything. You know that as well as I do. One of the scouts wandered off and got lost. The leaders decided that it was best to head back early. That's all."

Brad laughs. "Well, I know what everyone said, but I heard you were goofy as all get out. One of Jess's friends has been talking about it all summer. So, what was it, Jonboy? What did you do this time?"

I just shrug and walk away. Is he talking about Darla? Did Darla talk about me with Jess all summer?

I decide to shake it off. I am not going to let Brad get under my skin, not today. I could talk about the incident with the cat and Brad's car, but that just wouldn't be fair to Mr. Lemke, and I think the best response to bullying is to just walk away.

Finally, I spot Jess down the hall. She is chatting with a group of girls, all of them laughing and talking excitedly about their summer adventures.

I feel a pang of nervousness in my stomach. Marc was kind of right. There's that old feeling coming right back to me. I also kind of want to ask her what Darla might have said about me.

I raise a hand in a subdued wave, hoping she'll see me. Instead, Marc bumps me from behind and says, "I told you so." Then he turns and looks at me returning my sheepish wave and laughs.

Just as the first bell rings, I see a group of girls walk through the door down by Jess, and another screaming hug-fest happens. I guess it's not just first year high school girls who do that.

Marc pops me on the shoulder. "It's going to be quite the year. Let's go, superhero. You can pick your girl later."

I just shake my head and follow him in the other direction.

Shotgun

Darla

GADDY'S SITTING UP front with Mother, chatting away like they've known each other for years. It's almost impressive how quickly they've hit it off. Not that I mind—less focus on me and fewer awkward conversations.

They're all talking about it being the first day, and Mother insists on walking in with us to make sure the cousins get settled properly. Fine by me, as long as I don't have to endure her visit with Principal Douglas. I already know everything I need to know about this school. It's my first year here, too, but Jess and I have been texting, and I know exactly where to meet her.

As we drive through Grinwell, the conversation meanders through the typical landmarks. Olga points out the bowling alley, her eyes wide with mock amazement. "Wow, a real small-town bowling alley. How cute."

Gaddy giggles. "And look, there's an Applebee's. Fancy dining for a fancy town."

I smirk and mutter, "Don't knock it until you try it. You might be surprised, princess."

Mother shoots me a warning glance from the rearview mirror, but I ignore it. The cousins are loving this little tour of their new town, and honestly, so do I. It's almost enjoyable defending Grinwell, mostly because it allows me to at least feel like I am part of the conversation. I'm not sure how long Mother is going to allow this to go on, though, as her eyes are shooting out daggers right now.

So, of course, I will continue on.

I make up stories of haunted houses and gnarly murders that never really happened, but all my stories are based on movies I have seen. Yet, the girls take it all in ... until I mention one home where a teenager went missing and, years later, the rumor has it that a group of kids found a game that sucked them into another world. They immediately call me out on that one. How was I supposed to know they watched *Jumanji* where they are from? I thought that was just an American movie.

The talk inevitably turns to boys as we approach the school parking lot and see some of the guys walking toward the school.

"So, are the boys here any different from what we're used to, like them?" Olga asks, her tone dripping with curiosity as she points at some boys.

I'm not sure how I am supposed to respond to that, because I have no idea what they are "used to."

"Probably not," I reply. "You've got your jocks, nerds, troublemakers, and everything in-between. Just regular boys."

I really can't imagine it is different anywhere else in the world. Boys are boys. In reality, I would just as soon wrestle and pin them down than date them. It's just not my thing. At least, it hasn't been my thing.

"But they are good ol' boys from the Midwest," Gaddy adds with a snicker. "I bet they're all into trucks, football, and chewing tobacco."

Olga, ever the optimist, chimes in, "I think it's nice to be around some 'normal' people for a change."

I roll my eyes. "You're overselling the 'normal' part, Olga. And yes, they are very much into football. In fact, the whole town is into football. You would think it was a professional team by the way they treat the high school football team. It's incredibly annoying, to be honest. There are other sports and other teams, you know? Like wrestling."

Mother shoots me another dirty look.

Perfect, she heard me.

As we pull into the parking lot, the girls react to the school.

Gaddy says, "Well, we sure are in Kansas, aren't we, Toto?"

The other girls laugh at this, thinking it is funny, I guess, or not wanting to upset the Wicked Witch in the front seat.

It's true that Grinwell High School is on the edge of town and surrounded by cornfields, bean fields, hog farms, and the country. It's got a distinct smell that won't be mistaken for anything pleasant, that's for sure.

It's a brick building with glass front doors and signs everywhere, welcoming the Bluehill kids. Seeing as I come from Bluehill, it's nice to see they are making an effort to welcome us.

The school is much larger than Bluehill, but gauging from the reactions of my cousins, it doesn't impress them much.

Mother parks the Tahoe with the precision of an airplane pilot. I'm certain she is parked in a spot reserved for faculty, but she clearly doesn't care. She's determined to walk in with us, ensuring the cousins' registration is in order. Exactly what I need on my first day at a new school—walking in with my mother.

Gaddy jumps out of the car first, her fiery red hair catching the morning light like a beacon. She's dressed in a trendy outfit that screams, "Look at me." Seriously, it's like she thinks she's walking a red carpet instead of heading to school. Her presence is always larger than life and just adds to why I can't stand her.

Ronny follows close behind, flipping her blonde tips over her shoulder with as much attitude as anyone can muster before noon. She's wearing her usual leather jacket and jeans, looking like she's ready to take on the world, or start a revolution. It's all so "bad girl" cliché if you ask me.

Brenda, or Billow as we call her, climbs out next. Her perfectly styled brown hair looks like it's been through a salon, not a car ride. She's always in tight black leggings and a crop top, like she's about to hit the gym or strut down a runway. Billow is the master of distraction, always willing to make a scene out of nothing.

Heather, or Duff, with her sandy blonde hair and colorful California-style outfits, is next. She's got this uncanny ability to do impersonations, which can be entertaining but mostly annoying. The only one I enjoy is her impression of Mother; it's spot on and hilarious. She loves to dress in bright colors that make me want to put on sunglasses to look at her.

Katherine, or Hef, is hard to miss with her dark brown hair and her obsession with hot pink. She's a powerhouse of energy, always buzzing with positivity. Hef's like a walking battery charger—always boosting everyone around her with cheery comments. She tries that with me all the time—hard pass.

Olivia, or Liv, is the quiet one with her striking bleached-white hair and love for jumpsuits. She's got this weird ability to blend into the background, so much so that sometimes you forget she's even there. I can relate to that. In fact, I'd like to disappear right now.

Helga, or Olga, is the happy-go-lucky one with her soft, cool demeanor. Her blue outfits match her personality—calming and comforting. Olga is different from the rest, always trying to see the good in people. She's the only one of my cousins that seems half-normal. I could almost like her. Almost.

Lastly, there's Elanora, or Nora, with her black hair and blonde center part. She's over-the-top in everything she does, from her style to her personality. Nora's outfits are always shouting, "Help me." Today, she has on the tightest jeans I have ever seen. Good luck walking around in those all day.

Finally, I can back my way out of the Tahoe, once again humiliated by what can only look bizarre to any reasonable person. I feel the weight of a thousand eyes on us. It's hard not to notice a group of girls flanked by a mom on the first day of high school.

I scan the parking lot, hoping to spot a familiar face and make my escape. Then I see her—Jenny, my savior.

She shrieks with joy and rushes over, giving me the perfect opportunity to duck out of Mother's line of sight. "Darla! You made it."

"Jenny!" I exclaim, genuinely happy to see her. She is as stunning as I told her she would be and really is a sight for sore eyes after being effectively grounded all summer.

"So," she says, "are you going to introduce me to your cousins or what?" That's Jenny, one of the nicest people on the planet. She knows how difficult it has been for me with the cousins, but she can't help but be nice.

"Cousins, meet Jenny. Jenny, meet cousins."

Mother instantly puts her hands on her hips, and I know that my introduction was inadequate.

"Sorry, Jenny. This is Gaddy, Ronny, Billow, Duff, Hef, Liv, Nora, and Olga."

Jenny replies, "It's nice to meet all of you. Darla has told me so much about you. You are indeed a formidable group. All of you are gorgeous. Welcome to Blue—I mean, Grinwell, or whatever. I'm sure we will all be fast friends."

The cousins barely acknowledge her, and Gaddy says, "We are all the friends we need." Then she leads the pack, with Mother quickly stepping in behind them.

I linger behind with Jenny and mockingly whisper, "We are all the friends *we* need."

Yeah, great start, cousins. Great start.

Jenny and I quietly sneak off in the opposite direction of the office to explore some of the school and see if we can find Jess. I could text her, but I'm not so sure what the school rules are on cell phones. Besides, I'm interested in exploring a bit.

Locker Talk

Jon

MARC AND I MAKE OUR way to our lockers, which are conveniently located on the second floor. Grinwell High has this quirky setup where the freshmen are stuck on the top floor, giving them the longest walk. It's supposed to build character or something. Sophomores, juniors, and then seniors get progressively lower floors. Seniors have the easiest time with early dismissals and all, so it makes sense. Or, at least, that's my current working theory.

As we trudge up the stairs, Marc turns to me, smirking. "Ready for another year of this?"

I shrug. "As ready as I'll ever be."

We reach our lockers, and I fiddle with the combination lock, my mind drifting. It's nine to the right, twenty-one to the left, and then three to the right. Pull. *Argh.* I dig my phone out of my pocket to double-check my memory. Oh, four to the right. Got it.

This year feels different, heavier somehow. Maybe it is everything that happened last year, with Coach Locke and that whole mess. So much has changed that sometimes it is overwhelming.

I shake my head, trying to clear my thoughts. No time for that, not on the first day of school.

Just as the bell is about to ring again, a familiar crackle over the loudspeaker rings out as the warning of an incoming announcement. "*All students, please proceed to the gym for a school assembly. I repeat:*

all students, go to the gym. Grinwell kids, be sure to help the Bluehill students find their way."

"Typical first day stuff." Marc rolls his eyes. "Let's get this over with."

On our way down, we catch a glimpse of Sam and Taylor, a couple of guys from Bluehill. Sam is impossible to miss—a solid six-foot-four and must weigh over two hundred and twenty-five pounds, most of it muscle. He looks like he could have eaten a couple of our football players. His super curly hair and tan skin scream farm boy. It could also be his cowboy boots, which make him look even bigger. That's not a negative thing around here. If anything, it will bring him more immediate respect.

"Jon, Marc," Sam calls out, waving his massive hand. "Good to see you guys."

We walk toward them, and I say, "Hey, Sam and Taylor," nodding to both of them and offering a fist-bump. "Welcome to Grinwell. I mean, Grinwell-Bluehill, of course."

Taylor, who is about the same size as Marc, smiles. "Thanks, Jon. Good to be here."

As we start walking together, I glance at Sam. I can't shake the feeling that he might be the giant we are looking for. That would be a problem because it means he hasn't been registered with the APS. Grandpa, Marc, and I are on a mission to uncover who the giant, or giants, are. And, unfortunately, I need to figure out if Sam is one of them.

"So, what do you think of the school so far?" I ask Sam, trying to sound casual.

"Well, we just got here, but so far so good," Sam answers, looking around. "Big change from Bluehill, not that it's a bad thing."

Marc says, "Jon and I have been in Grinwell schools since kindergarten. We know almost everyone, and they all know us. That's both good and bad, but I have to admit it's nice that we were able to keep going to our school and didn't have to switch. That has to be harder for you guys."

"It's not too bad," Sam says. "I met Taylor in sixth grade when my family moved to Bluehill. Before that, I lived in Ballard, Utah, on a ranch. I went to school on the reservation there. Talk about different. Making that change was harder than I think this one will be. Life on the reservation was so different from here. So, I'm not too worried."

Taylor jumps in, grinning, "Sam's great-grandfather was a Navajo chief. Isn't that cool?"

I nod in agreement, making a mental note to research Navajo legends and ask Grandpa about them. "That's really interesting. We've been here our whole lives, like Marc said, so if you need anything, just let us know." I cringe a little because that may have come out like we think we are better than them, which isn't true at all. We just know how the school works and, for whatever reason, the staff and everyone seems to like Marc and I. Probably because we are somewhat nerds, but there is value in that, for sure, because the staff can be super helpful.

As we walk, we pass by the trophy cases lining the hallway. Marc points to one of the cases. "Remember that game last year when we won the district championship? Feels like ages ago."

"I remember," Sam says. "You guys were really good last year. We were just such a small team that most of us had to play both offense and defense, so we were gassed by the end of the game. It's going to be nice to have more players, for sure, although I do like playing on both sides of the ball."

We continue down the hall, passing by plaques dedicated to Coach Keith, our old PE teacher and wrestling coach. The official story is that he was killed by a large animal, but Marc and I know better. It was Coach Locke, the misguided and pure evil descendant of Loki, who killed him.

Coach Locke was hunting for sources of blue essence and targeted Grinwell because of me. Well, he didn't know it was me, and that was part of the problem. He was convinced that Marc was a descendant of Thor and kidnapped him to steal his blue essence, which is what gives all of us descendants our powers. I managed to defeat him and save Marc, but the memory still haunts me, quite literally. And then Coach Locke used a troll cross to come back as a draugr—aka ghost—and attack me again over the summer …

Deep in thought, I almost run over a group of lost students.

Marc nudges me. "You okay?"

"Yeah, just thinking." I shake my head. "Sorry, let's keep moving."

We finally make it to the gym, which is buzzing with excitement on the first day. The bleachers are filling up fast, but we manage to find seats at the top, near the middle. Sam and Taylor sit with us, and I notice a few more familiar faces from Bluehill joining us.

Principal Douglas steps up to the microphone, tapping it to get everyone's attention. "Welcome back, students, to another exciting year at Grinwell and now Bluehill High. I hope you all had a fantastic summer. Today, we're going to go over some basic rules and housekeeping, and I'd like to introduce our new teachers."

Marc leans over and whispers, "Bet we're getting another new PE teacher and wrestling coach."

I nod. "Probably. I mean, we don't have one. Let's hope this one lasts."

"And that they aren't a murdering giant from Hades," Marc adds.

I give him a quick look, which he immediately recognizes as a "keep your voice down" plea. He nods then shrugs an apology.

"So, what's first on your schedule today?" I ask Sam.

"Math, then English," he replies. "You?"

"Oh, mine is the opposite. I have English then Calculus."

Taylor pipes up, "Dang, that's a bummer. It would have been an easier start to the day with people we know."

"Totally," Marc agrees.

As we sit there, I feel a strange sense of camaraderie. Despite the mission to uncover the giant, I can't help but like Sam. He is genuine, and his presence is comforting in a way I didn't expect. It's like we have been friends forever.

That reminds me. I pull out my phone and discreetly start running searches on Google about Navajo's in Utah. The first thing that comes up is Skinwalker Ranch. Now that is something that I forgot about. I remember reading legends about UFO activity in that area and all kinds of other strange happenings, some of which are rooted in Navajo folklore regarding people that can take on animal forms. That gets my mind wandering, and I completely don't pay attention to whatever Principal Douglas is saying.

I send Grandpa a quick text, as that is something that we are going to want to discuss tonight. "*Is there any known relationship between giants and Native American skinwalkers or possibly aliens?*" Actually, I never really asked Grandpa about aliens but, at this point, after dealing with so much, I can literally believe anything is possible.

Getting Jumped

Darla

JENNY AND I MAKE OUR way to our lockers, chatting about our schedules and the teachers we hope to avoid this year. As I open my locker to put my bookbag in, someone jumps on my back, screaming.

"Hey, Jess. Get off, please," I say, barely able to hold back. Today is not a good day to mess with me.

Jess clings to me for a moment longer before hopping down. "How did you know it was me?"

Jenny answers for me, "Because you're about the only other girl we know, and certainly the only one who does that to Darla. Which is hilarious because, if anyone else did that, they'd be thrown onto the floor as fast as they jumped on."

Jess blinks, looking genuinely surprised. "I didn't realize you didn't like that. We've been doing it for so long in dance that it just feels natural."

"It's not a big deal." I shrug. "But, yeah, it would be great if a hug was the signature greeting going forward."

Jess looks apologetic. "I'm sorry, Darla. I had no idea."

An awkward silence falls over us, so I give Jess a look and say, "Honestly, I am just always happy to see you. I really don't care it's just different, but different isn't always bad. Are we good?"

Jess smiles, the tension dissolving, and then, with renewed vigor, she says, "Deal. Hugs from now on."

We all laugh it off and quickly move on.

"Jess, you remember Jenny, right?" I ask.

Jess says, "Of course, I do. Jenny, you look amazing today. Welcome officially to Grinwell Bluehill High."

Jenny, clearly happy with the compliment, timidly replies, "Thanks, Jess. I appreciate that."

I give Jess a look, indicating that was nicely done and that I also appreciate the welcome.

Just then, there is an unusual parting of the sea of students in the hall that catches my attention. My cousins are walking toward us, and it seems like every boy in the hallway is nearly drooling over them. *Gross.* They soak up the attention, clearly loving every bit of it. A little too much, if you ask me.

Gaddy struts up first. "Mother says you should show us around."

What's this? They are going to be calling *her* Mother now, as well? Yeah, that registers. That said, it's going to make things weird if they say that around everyone. For now, I let that slide and mockingly say, "*Mother says you should show us around.*" Then I follow with, "Well, Mother isn't here, is she?"

As if I didn't say anything, Gaddy says, "Yeah, well, whatever. Let's get on with it."

I just reply, "How does that even make sense? I'm new to this school, as well."

Jess can't stay quiet any longer and jumps in, saying, "Hi, I'm Jess. I'm the head cheerleader, and I would love to show you around. Do any of you cheer? Do you dance, like Darla? Do you play any sports, like Darla?" The questions come fast, furious, and full of fun and excitement. "By the way, which of you is Gaddy?" she asks like she already knows because, of course, I have been texting her about my cousins and described them fairly well or, at least, I would like to think I did.

They all look at me, so I do the introductions. "Jess, meet Gaddy, Ronny, Billow, Duff, Hef, Liv, Nora, and Olga. Cousins, meet Jess.

Jess is one of my best friends and also belongs to my dance company. We have spent many hours together on the dance floor, so be nice.." I purposefully deliver this with as little passion as possible just to make sure all of them know that I do not enjoy any part of this. I'm so over all of it.

They start to shake hands, but Jess has none of that. She hugs each one, saying their name as she does, as if to lock them into her memory. "Welcome to Grinwell, everyone. Any relative of Darla's is a friend of mine. Let me show you around."

We walk through the halls as Jess points out all the important spots—restrooms, lunchroom, and library. We reached the area where the cheerleaders practice in the old gym. The school has two gyms—the new gym for volleyball and basketball teams, and the old gym dominated by cheerleading, dance, and some of the unofficial clubs.

Jess makes sure to point out the sign-up forms for the cheerleading team and dance team. "You guys would be a great fit for either team. You're clearly in great shape. It's a really great way to exercise and, of course, meet boys. Although, I can already see you aren't going to have any problems in that department."

She then leads us to an area in the old gym with mats on the floor and a big pit full of foam pieces. She takes a running start and does every kind of flip known to man before landing in the foam pit. Crawling out, she proclaims, "That's how it's done, ladies."

Gaddy rolls her eyes and proceeds to do the exact same routine, jumping out of the pit and brushing off her shoulders. Then, with her hands on her hips, she proclaims, "Too easy. What else can you do?"

Jess grins, and challenges back, "Show up for tryouts and find out. Well, this tour isn't going to move itself, ladies. Keep walking."

I can't help but admire Jess. She is amazing and completely unfazed by Gaddy's behavior. I love that about her. It must be nice to have that much confidence. Although, she is also the best in the school, so that helps.

As we exit the old gym, we run into Brad and what appears to be the entire line of the football team. It is a bunch of large boys with Brad walking in the center of all of them. It almost looks like a roaming huddle coming down the hallway toward us, with no other students anywhere to be seen.

Jess walks up to him and jumps into his arms, giving him a big hug. "My hero!" She then proceeds to introduce Brad and the football players to the cousins one by one, getting their names perfect. Of course.

Brad looks to Jess. "I was looking for you."

Jess asks, "Why?"

"Jess, didn't you hear the announcement Principal Douglas made over the intercom?"

Jess explains, "Well, we were in the old gym, and the speakers in there don't work. So no, what did we miss?"

"We are supposed to make our way to the new gym for an announcement."

"They really need to fix the speakers in the old gym. It's ridiculous."

"We're going to be late, so let's go."

Jess and Brad lead the way as the rest of us follow. It feels strange but powerful to have such a large group of girls walking in near unison to the gym, led by a football team. It definitely draws attention. That can be good or bad, but it oddly feels right to me.

As we walk, I find myself thinking about how different this year is going to be—the new school, the cousins, being with both Jenny and Jess every day.

As we get closer to the gym, I see pictures from last year's Grinwell teams still up on the wall—the football team, basketball team, volleyball team, and wrestling team. I nearly freeze in place at the sight of Coach Locke and Dustin, as memories of scout camp come rushing back to me. I have never in my life been that afraid, and I will never be that afraid ever again. No way.

Jenny notices me looking at the wrestling poster and says, "Still chasing that dream?"

"What dream?" I wonder if she actually remembers what happened at camp this summer. Is it possible that her memory came back?

"The dream of getting on the wrestling team, silly."

"Oh, yeah," I reply. "I'm definitely going to try out for wrestling this year, one hundred percent."

Jess clears her throat. "Uh, um, girls, the assembly isn't going to wait for us."

With that, we walk into the assembly, and the bleachers are full of students. In fact, it has already begun because there is a man standing at the microphone.

He says, "So nice of you to join us, Mr. Dillon." As if some magical power is being used, the students clear a spot for Brad and Jess to sit, and then the space keeps expanding for all of us. It must be nice to have this much power over everyone. For now, I accept this and just grab a seat between Jess and Jenny.

Assembly

Jon

SAM PULLS ME AWAY FROM my thoughts about skinwalkers, peppering me with more questions. Apparently, I'm not the only one who has trouble listening to Principal Douglas drone on and on. I would rather just read whatever he's saying and be done with it in half the time. Usually, if you boil what he is saying down to the truly important points, it would fit on half a sheet of paper, at most. Instead, he will take at least twenty minutes talking about gardens, forests, new adventures, and whatnot.

"Hey, Jon," Sam whispers, leaning closer. "What's the deal with all these different groups of kids sitting together? Looks like everyone has their own little clique."

"Yeah, it's pretty typical," I reply, scanning the bleachers. "The sports teams usually sit together. See over there? The basketball players, tall and lanky, are huddled together, no doubt discussing whatever the latest NBA rumor happens to be."

The wrestling team is a mix of muscular and wiry guys, their connection evident in their casual punches, shoves, pointing, and laughter. Farther down, the track team is a blend of lean athletes that scream of stamina and large people that are capable of throwing objects long distances. The band kids are easily recognizable, well, because they have their instruments. So, apparently, they are going to be playing something. The choir kids are grouped together; generally speaking, they are the most attentive, as if they are viewing a vocal performance. The cheerleaders and dance team are mostly one in the same, at least they were at Grinwell. Jill is sitting with them since she knows many of them from her dance company. The chess club is quieter and more reserved, and if Sam wasn't with Marc and I, we probably would be sitting with them.

Sam nods, taking it all in. "Makes sense. At Bluehill, it was pretty much the same." He starts pointing out some kids he recognizes from Bluehill, exchanging waves with a few of them. It's clear they all know Sam and seem to wish they could be sitting by him. The guy is like a human magnet.

I normally don't use my powers at school. It's too risky, and I have to be careful. But I have to find something out.

I pull out my phone and look up one of the rhymes from the *Book of Bragi* that Grandpa gave me. The book doesn't contain specific rhymes to recite word for word. Instead, it has concepts that a Bragi can use to manipulate any living thing. There are rhymes for just about anything. Unfortunately, there isn't one for a big red arrow pointing at any giants in the room. However, there is one that will uncover any magic in the area. It reads, *"Mention your surroundings and the people you want to check in the area and relate that to some appropriate sound or sounds."*

Okay. I think about it for a minute, and then I whisper quietly, barely moving my lips:

"As I look around this room, full of strangers and friends,
   I find the need to explore, looking for magical trends.
   If some giants are present, please give me some signs;
   Make sure the next applause is one that perfectly aligns."

As soon as Principal Douglas hands the microphone over to Mr. Sperry, the new PE/wrestling coach, the students erupt into synchronized clapping. It's definitely strange and clearly a sign that magic is present in the room. It might not be a giant, but there is magic, nonetheless.

Mr. Sperry assumes this is for him, so he turns to look at Principal Douglas, who shrugs and turns to the crowd to take a bow. He then is back to the microphone. "Thank you. Thank you very much."

Marc leans over to me and whispers, "That was you, wasn't it?"

I nod. Marc knows me too well. "Yes, I'll tell you later," I mutter under my breath.

Sam, who has been watching the synchronized clapping with a puzzled look but trying to fall in line, turns to me. "Does your school always clap in unison? Is that a Grinwell thing or something?"

"No, it's not normal," I say quickly. "It looks like maybe the football team started it. The school generally goes along with whatever they do." I point over to where Brad is sitting, surrounded by his entourage of players, each one looking more pumped than the last. Brad, with his perfectly tousled hair and broad shoulders, epitomizes the all-American football hero.

"Yeah, I know Dillon," Sam says, nodding toward Brad. "We played Grinwell last year, and he scored five touchdowns on us." Sam goes into some football lingo, talking about plays and stats, which loses me a little, but the point is clear—Brad is a great football player, and everyone in Bluehill knows of him.

"After the assembly, I'll introduce you," I tell Sam.

"Thanks, bro. I appreciate it. You're all right, Bragg."

I cringe internally at the thought. No doubt, Brad is going to lay into me in front of Sam and Taylor, just because he can. But I push the thought aside for now.

The assembly drags on, with Mr. Sperry handing the microphone back to Principal Douglas and him going through the usual first-day housekeeping as promised.

My mind drifts back to the synchronized clapping. There is definitely magic here, but what kind? Who is using it?

I glance around the room, trying to spot anyone who looks out of place or overly focused. But everyone seems normal. Too normal.

I spend most of the rest of the assembly sneaking peeks at Darla. I am not sure if she sees me or not. I think she does, but she could just be looking over at Sam and Taylor. It's really hard to say. She looks really good, though. I know that.

My mind drifts back into the tunnels under the burial ground where the troll crosses were placed. I remember seeing her there and how scared she was. She was so happy to see me. Yet, she unfortunately had to witness the battle between Coach Locke and myself. In the end, it worked out, but it didn't look good there for a while. I don't think I am ever going to be able to get that out of my mind, and all I really want to do is to protect her. I would go to great lengths to make sure she never has to experience anything like that again.

Seeing as she is sitting with Jess and, therefore, Brad, that is going to add to my nervousness as I walk over to introduce Sam to Brad. I just can't help but get a little tongue-tied around her, and I guess Brad, too, for that matter, for completely different reasons. I actually care what Darla thinks about me, and I long since gave up caring about what Brad thinks.

The school fight song—or should I say, songs—play one at a time. First, the Grinwell fight song, with its upbeat tempo and familiar lyrics that bring back memories of pep rallies and school spirit. Then the Bluehill one, with its more traditional, almost militaristic rhythm, meant to instill a sense of pride and discipline. That quickly makes it clear where everyone is from.

After both songs play, Mr. Douglas announces a contest for naming our new mascot of the combined Grinwell-Bluehill High School as well as a separate contest for writing the school fight song.

Marc elbows me. "Jon, you should enter to write the school fight song."

"I don't know. I'm not sure that is a good idea." I think to myself that I'm actually not even sure what might happen if I did that. In fact, I'm almost positive other Bragi have gotten in trouble over time for doing exactly that. I'll confirm that with Grandpa tonight, but I know someone mentioned that. Maybe it was Coach Locke? Yikes, just thinking about him sends shivers up my spine.

Finally, the assembly ends, and we all stand up and stretch our legs. Then I lead Sam, Taylor, and Marc over to where Brad and his group are hanging out. Brad sees us coming and raises an eyebrow.

As soon as we get over there, Jenny is already embracing Sam and Taylor. She is just as excited to see them as Jill was to see her friends—jumping, screaming, and all the usual fun—but the sound is absorbed by all of the students leaving the assembly.

Darla gives Sam a fist-bump, and as I get closer to her, my heart starts pumping really hard, and I find myself getting more and more excited.

"Hey, Brad," I say, trying to keep my voice steady. "This is Sam. He's new here, from Bluehill."

The Parting

Darla

AFTER THE ASSEMBLY, everyone seems to converge on Brad and Jess, snapping pictures with them like they are celebrities. I can't help but roll my eyes at the scene.

Olga turns to me, looking puzzled. "What's that all about?"

"Brad is the quarterback of the football team, and Jess is the head cheerleader," I explain. "So, they're basically royalty here at Grinwell."

"*Ooo*, royalty. That sounds interesting," Olga replies. Then she thinks about it for a second and looks even more confused. "But there isn't a quarterback in football."

I laugh. "American football, not European."

"Ah, right. American football. I've never seen a game but have heard about it. This year is going to be something special. I can just feel it. Don't worry about tonight; it's going to be fun."

Jenny, who has been listening, asks, "What's happening tonight?"

I give her a shrug and puzzled look. "I'll tell you later."

As I watch the commotion around Brad and Jess, my thoughts drift to Coach Sperry. He's a short man with a full mustache and a weathered exterior, the kind of guy who looks like he's seen it all. I'm trying to remember where he wrestled—was it the University of Iowa or Iowa State? Either way, he has a ton of experience, and I'm looking forward to meeting him.

It's not easy for a girl to get on any of the boys' teams, even now. There's so much resistance, especially in wrestling, because of the close proximity to the boys. Not that I care about any of that. I'd just as soon throw them on the ground than hold them in an embrace. Hopefully, Mr. Sperry is a progressive and reasonable coach who understands that girls deserve to be able to do anything boys can do.

I look around, hoping to catch a glimpse of Coach Sperry, but I see that he's heading out with the rest of the faculty. This probably isn't the right time to try to talk to him, anyway.

I realize I've wandered off a bit from Jenny and Jess. As I look back, I see Jenny embracing Sam and Taylor and head back over to them to say hello.

"Hey, guys, welcome to Grinwell, right?" I say, smiling.

Sam and Taylor grin back. "We haven't seen you since scout camp," Sam says.

"Yeah, I've been really busy and living out being grounded because of the 'incident.' Mother took away my phone, so it's been a bit difficult to keep in touch with everyone."

"Over you getting lost at camp?" Sam asks, raising an eyebrow. "That's kind of harsh, isn't it? I mean, even for your mom."

"Well, you know Mother," I reply, shrugging. "Plus, my cousins came to stay with us this year." With that, I introduce Sam and Taylor to them all. "Sam and Taylor, meet Gaddy, Ronny, Billow, Duff, Hef, Liv, Nora, and Olga. Cousins, meet Sam and Taylor. They are a couple of my best friends from Bluehill" I'm really getting tired of this already, as well as the surprised looks I get from everyone. I mean, it is weird; they're not wrong. Why did so many of my "cousins" come to visit? Exactly how many aunts and uncles do I have? I wish I knew the answer to that, but honestly, I just don't care.

"Greetings, ladies. Welcome to Bluehill-Grinwell," Sam says with a friendly wave.

Brad, of course, has to barge over and blurt out, "It's Grinwell-Bluehill."

Just then, Jon steps between them and says, "Brad, meet Sam. Sam, meet Brad."

Brad and Sam stare at each other for a minute, the whole Grinwell versus Bluehill thing playing out before our eyes.

Then Sam breaks the staring contest and says, "Right, Grinwell-Bluehill, gals. Welcome to Grinwell-Bluehill High School." He says that without his eyes leaving Brad's. It's one of those out-of-the-side-of-your-mouth acknowledgments but also clearly indicates he isn't going to submit to Brad.

Brad reaches out his fist, and Sam gives it a bump.

"Good to meet you, QB1," Sam says.

Brad seems to recognize Sam, as well. "Yeah, all of us have been looking forward to having you on the team. Definitely beats having to go against you. What did you have—twenty tackles against us last year?"

"Fifteen and two sacks, QB1. You still managed to score five touchdowns," Sam replies with a grin.

With that, Brad seems satisfied, and the guys on the football team each take turns giving Sam a bro-hug or locking hands in some sort of bro-shake. It's too much testosterone for my taste. The entire scene looks like a pack of wolves greeting a new alpha. *Ugh.*

Right at that point, Mr. Douglas walks over and tells us, "Get to class, kids."

We exchange eye rolls and start to make our way toward the gym exit. As we walk, we pass under banners hanging from the gym ceiling. Grinwell has won the conference championships in football the last two years, and there are dozens of banners from over the last several years. There are also a bunch of displays on the wall, showing all of the school record holders and stats from last year. The cousins can't help but notice that Brad Dillon's name appears several times.

Olga says, "I can see why everyone is so infatuated with Brad."

"Exactly."

As we move toward the hallway, still surrounded by admirers, the speakers continue to drone on about how this day is a brand-new start for both schools and is surely going to be one to remember. The day that the two became one and would dominate the conference, etc. All of this is met with cheers and jeers from the students. It's clear that drumming up combined school spirit is going to be a recurring theme for a while.

Olga leans closer to me and whispers, "This place is really big on sports, huh?"

I nod. "Yeah, they take it pretty seriously. But it's not just about sports. There's a lot of pride in the schools—I mean, school."

We continue walking, and I watch my cousins taking it all in. Liv's eyes are practically popping out of her head as she stares at the trophy case, probably having never seen so many sports awards in one place. Gaddy looks like she's ready to take on the world, scanning the hallways like she's already planning her next move. Billow is glued to her phone, probably documenting every little thing as if she's on some kind of school safari.

It's a lot to process, especially on the first day—the noise, the crowds, the smell of old textbooks mixed with various locker odors. It's a sensory overload.

Duff is already trying to chat up some random students, flashing her bright smile and tossing her blonde hair like she's in a shampoo commercial. Hef is practically vibrating with energy, looking like she might burst into a cheer routine at any second as the students respond to the intercom rah-rah. Nora is doing her usual "look at me" routine, making sure she's noticed by everyone we pass.

Olga, though, is the one who surprises me. She's genuinely curious, taking in every detail with wide-eyed wonder, like she's discovering a new world. She's the only one who doesn't seem fazed by the chaos. She even smiles at a few passing students, trying to make a connection. It would be almost endearing, if I didn't find this whole situation so annoying.

I almost feel a pang of empathy for them—thrown into this crazy new environment with no idea how things work. They're out of their element, and it's kind of amusing to watch them flounder. But then I quickly snap out of that. They've disrupted my life enough, invading my space and turning everything upside down. Let them deal with the chaos and confusion. It's about time they got a taste of what it feels like to be an outsider.

As we near the exit, Jenny pulls me aside. "So, what's happening tonight?"

I glance around to make sure no one is listening. "I really don't know. My mother has something planned for me and the cousins. I'm sure it will be a massive waste of time and that I will manage to get into more trouble with Mother. I'm not looking forward to it."

Jenny's eyes light up with curiosity. "Would it help if I came?"

"I wish," I say. "Sadly, this is one I'm going to have to do on my own. Trust me; if I could get out of going, I would literally do anything else, but Mother insists."

We rejoin the group and make our way to our classes. This is a first day like none of us have ever had before. We really don't know what to expect. Which is kind of annoying because, at our individual schools, we had the routine down. Now, we have to learn how to deal with this all over again—new classrooms, new teachers, and new kids to get comfortable around. Oh well, might as well get used to it.

Big Brother

Jon

PART OF THE ASSEMBLY that I apparently wasn't paying attention to at all was a plea from Mr. Douglas that the Grinwell students help the Bluehill students navigate the halls and get to class.

We are still in a bunch, with Brad and Sam leading the charge. Brad takes the lead, asking, "Who has math now? You can follow me." Then, looking at our books, he says, "Who has English? You can follow ... Bragg. Yep, nobody knows how to get to Mr. Young's class better than Bragg. Just make sure your nose isn't buried in a book the whole way, Bragg."

Everyone laughs, and I don't really know why. It's the kind of laugh you do when someone you really admire wants you to laugh at something they said. It's kind of a pity laugh, but the jokes on them really, because I do love English class and I don't really care at all who knows that.

I see that Darla is in the group heading to English, so I make my way over to her through the pack of football players and her cousins. As I am passing Brad, I feel a pull on my leg from behind, and I come crashing into Darla, taking her down with me. My face immediately burns red. I can't believe he just did that. Of course, Brad is already laughing, thinking he is the funniest person on earth.

"Whoa, careful there, tiger. Bragg, we know you are head-over-heels for Darla, but this is over the top, even for you. At least ask her out on a date next time," Brad shouts, his voice dripping with mockery.

As I am sprawled on the floor, I can see Darla's eyes widen in surprise. The crowd around us erupts in laughter, the sound echoing off the hall walls.

My mind races, trying to process the embarrassment. I must have stayed down a few seconds too long, looking into Darla's eyes. Suddenly, I feel someone grab me from behind, lifting me up and setting me on my feet. It happens so fast that all I can do is mouth the word "*Sorry*" in Darla's direction. Then I turn around and back up a step to see that it was Sam.

"You okay?" Sam asks.

I just nod and can't help but put my head down. The whole thing was a bit too embarrassing. Not what Brad said—I can ignore him easily enough. I am more worried about looking like a klutz again in front of Darla.

After also helping Darla up, Sam then does something unexpected. He turns his attention to Brad and says, "Dillon, that wasn't cool."

Well, that's interesting. I pull my head up to see this exchange.

Brad shrugs, his expression feigning innocence. "I have no idea what you're talking about."

"We all saw you trip Jon. Where we come from, that's some bullcrap. Why don't you leave him alone? Jon's a good guy. By the way, y'all going to English are lucky to have him leading you to class. Is anyone else going to math class? I don't want to follow Dillon. I don't appreciate how he leads."

A short, thin boy—I think it is Dwayne Surber—barely visible behind the football players, raises his hand.

Sam gives him a fist-bump and heads off with him, but then he turns around and says, "See you at lunch, Jon."

Brad, taking this all in, just says, "Geez, Bragg, tell your big brother to take a chill pill. I'm just having some fun with you."

More laughs follow, but they are less robust this time.

Brad leads them in the direction Sam went then turns and says, "See you at lunch, Bragg." After a long pause, he adds, "*Not.*"

The slight giggling fades as they walk away.

I start to lead everyone going to English class, but a bunch of them have already left, leaving Marc, Darla, Olga—I think that's her cousin's name—and a few others. I repeat my apology to Darla, and then we head off.

As we are walking, Darla says, "Sam's right. Brad is a jerk. I don't see what Jess sees in him. Anyone who acts like that is not someone I want to be around. How long have you put up with that guy?"

"He wasn't always like that," I reply. "In elementary school, Marc, Brad, and I were all good friends. We were inseparable. We went to cub scouts and hung out every day. Everything started changing in junior high when Brad immediately became a football hero. That's when Jess and he started dating, as well. For whatever reason, he made it his life's mission to give me a hard time. Jokes on him, though, because I don't really care. You're right, though, Sam's great. I'm glad he's here. Hopefully, he will rub off on Brad some."

I glance at Marc, who gives me a supportive nod.

"Yeah, we used to have a lot of fun together," Marc chimes in. "We'd play video games at Jon's house, have sleepovers, and ride our bikes all over town. We even had a secret clubhouse in the woods where we'd hang out and make plans for our imaginary adventures. He was just one of us back then."

I give Marc a look that means *really?* He just waves it off.

We walk through the crowded hallways, and I point out some of the landmarks of Grinwell High. "Over there's the library. Mrs. Snow is the librarian. She's pretty cool; lets you check out as many books as you want. It's one of the best spots in the school if you ever need a quiet place to think."

Darla nods, looking interested. "I might have to check that out. With everything going on at the farm, it's hard to find a place to be alone. I'm sure that is going to make homework difficult."

"Mr. Young's class is great, too. He always finds interesting books for us to read. He makes English a lot more fun than you'd expect. Of course, Brad's right; I do love reading, so I am inherently biased."

As I continue talking, I get completely lost in the conversation with Darla and almost forget that I am leading everyone to Mr. Young's class. I literally walk past it and have to turn the group around to go back a couple of doors.

"Sorry, guys. Mr. Young's class is back here," I say, feeling a bit sheepish.

As we enter the classroom, I notice that Mr. Young is wearing a Viking helmet, which is totally unexpected. He greets everyone as we come in, saying "Heil og sæl" or "heill ok sæll," and then in English, "Be happy and healthy." I do know that some people say that is how the Norse would greet each other, but I'm not totally sure about that. It's kind of a strange greeting, right? Why not just say hello?

Even though I am caught off guard, I just reply, "Right back at you, Mr. Young."

We all grab seats and notice a book on each one. I am somewhat familiar with it already, and a wave of excitement washes over me.

Mr. Young always has a knack for picking out the best reads. This time, I am going to get to read something about my ancestors, which is about as good as it gets. Plus, I know a ton about it now after all of my training with the APS and Grandpa.

Darla sits down close to the front of the class, and I can see her curiosity piqued by the book, or maybe it is disdain. I guess I can't tell yet. Whatever it is, she reacts to seeing it and reads the cover.

Marc, sitting on the other side of me, leans over and whispers, "Did you say something to Mr. Young? Why did he pick this book? Did he recently stream *Ragnarök* on Netflix or something? Or maybe he's been binge-watching *Vikings* or *The Last Kingdom*? Heck, he could even be a closet Marvel fan and just watched *Thor: Ragnarök* for the tenth time."

I chuckle. "Maybe. Whatever it was, Mr. Young does seem to be fully committed to it with that helmet."

Mr. Young, having overheard us, smiles and says, "You'll have to wait and see, Marc. This year's reading list has some surprises. Plus, I am always fully committed to literature. You of all people should know that, Jon. It's the only way to truly appreciate fine works of art."

As the rest of the class settles in, I feel a strange sense of comfort. Despite the morning's chaos, sitting in Mr. Young's class feels like a return to normalcy.

I glance over at Darla, who is flipping through the book. It is nice having her here, someone who understands the craziness that our lives sometimes entail. At a minimum, I am going to have something to talk about with her every day since we will be reading the same book. Unless she hates it, and then we can discuss why she feels that way.

Jotnar Myths

Darla

CLASS STARTS WITH MR. Young introducing himself. He stands at the front of the room, his Viking helmet still perched on his head. He's a pretty large man with reddish hair, round glasses, and a mustache that makes him look a bit like I would imagine a movie or food critic would look like.

"Good morning, everyone. I'm Mr. Young, and I've been teaching at Grinwell High for ten years now. Today, I'd like to get to know all of you better. So, let's go around the room, and please tell us where you went to school last year and something you enjoy doing—a hobby, a passion, anything."

Being near the front, I know I'll have to go early. When it's my turn, I stand up and say, "Darla Towns, Bluehill. I enjoy wrestling." I just want to get this over with as fast as possible.

That gets some surprised looks, including one from Mr. Young.

"Very well," he says, clearly intrigued. "We have a pretty great wrestling team here at Grinwell. I think they have a cheer team, as well. Next."

I jump in, "Oh, I intend to wrestle, Mr. Young."

There are a few snickers and lots of surprised looks.

Mr. Young, taking that in quickly, replies, "How interesting. Good for you, Darla. I think that's great. Then I'll be happy to cheer for you."

Olga gives me a look like she wants to ask me something, but she's next. Mr. Young points at her, and she stands up confidently.

"Olga, from Norway. I enjoy swimming and anything that involves being around water."

Mr. Young nods appreciatively. "We have a swim team you might want to check out."

As more students introduce themselves, I start to notice a pattern. Every time someone mentions an interest, Mr. Young points out a related sport, club, or activity at Grinwell-Bluehill High, making sure to mention both towns every time. I start to drift off a bit, letting my mind wander.

It was nice talking to Jon earlier. I glance back to see if he is looking my way and, of course, he is. His head snaps away just as I catch his eye. I guess that's something we're going to be doing when we have class together. I think I'm going to have some fun with that.

Honestly, I'm still not totally sure how I feel about him. I've never had a boyfriend before—wait, let's not get ahead of ourselves. I can't believe I even thought that. I really don't know him that well, and I need to focus on school, the farm, and trying to make the wrestling team. Still, I can't stop thinking about him.

Next up is Marc, who stands up and says, "Marc. Grinwell. I enjoy playing video games."

Mr. Young smiles. "Video games, you say. There's a gaming club here you might be interested in, but I'm pretty sure you and Jon are already in it, right?"

Then it's Jon's turn. He stands up, looking a bit shy. "Jon. Grinwell. I like reading."

Mr. Young beams. "Perfect place for you then, Jon. I know you're going to enjoy this class. We are going to explore all kinds of new worlds and go on many adventures together this year through some of the best books on different cultures. At Grinwell-Bluehill, we are all about inclusion and being aware of what makes us all different and the common threads we all share."

The introductions continue, each student sharing a bit about themselves, and Mr. Young enthusiastically points them to even more various clubs and activities. I guess it's his way to try to point everyone in the right direction. I'm sure some find that useful, but I know exactly what I want to do this year, even if it will drive Mother crazy. Actually, especially if it will drive Mother crazy.

I think back to this summer when Mother and I had one of our many disagreements. It was right after the incident at scout camp, and Mother decided that I needed to focus on more "ladylike" activities. She was going on about how young women should be in the arts, doing dance or cheerleading. "Darla," she said in that stern voice of hers, "young women should not be tangled up with sweaty, smelly boys on a mat, trying to pin them down or escaping from them."

Her words still ring in my ears. I remember standing there, fists clenched, trying to keep my cool. "Mother, wrestling is just as much of an art as dance. It's about strategy, strength, and discipline. Plus, I enjoy it. Isn't that what matters? Besides, how is doing all of the chores on the farm and around the house 'ladylike?'"

Mother looked at me like I had grown another head. "What matters is that you present yourself as a proper young lady. Wrestling is not for girls like you, and hard work is just as important for ladies as it is gentlemen."

That was the last straw. I stormed out of the room, slamming the door behind me.

It's not just about wrestling; it's about everything. Mother wants to mold me into her image of the perfect daughter, and I want to break free of that mold.

Just as I am getting lost in that internal conversation, Olga leans over and whispers, "Have you read this book before?"

"Um, no. Have you?"

"Yeah. Actually, it was required reading at my house."

"Really? Why?"

Olga smiles mysteriously. "Well, one, because I am from Norway, and two, you'll find out tonight."

"Great, can't wait," I quip, but honestly, that makes no sense to me. What could tonight possibly have to do with this book?

Sensing my tone, Olga says, "Seriously, give it a chance. Also, does Mother know that you want to wrestle?"

I just throw up my hands in surrender, forgetting for a moment that I am in class.

Mr. Young notices. "Perfect, thanks, Darla. Please start reading."

After stumbling looking for the page number, I end up having to ask Mr. Young.

He says, "You're going to want to pay attention, or you might get lost in a strange new world."

I just nod to indicate I understand and turn to where Mr. Young says and read the following:

> "*Hail to the Lady and Lord of the Sea,*
> *That greet sailors that come to thee,*
> *As they offer you up tokens of gold.*
> *Keep them safe from the waters so cold,*
> *To the Lord known by the Gods to be true,*
> *As he treats them to his glorious brew.*
> *Known for his benevolence and love of all,*
> *Aegir fill our nets with a bountiful haul.*
> *Keep Ran calm and under your firm control,*
> *Lest she lure us all in her fatal thrall,*
> *And drags us with her net to depths below,*
> *Where we will be lost forever, as you know.*
> *May your nine daughters that come in waves,*
> *Treat us like sailors and not as slaves.*

Blodughadda with her bloody hair and anger,
Dufa with her pitching wave and clangor,
Bylgja with her billows that will distract,
Hefring whose rising wave makes all react,
Himinglaeva who is transparent and still,
Hronn whose welling wave swells our tears,
Kolga whose cool wave chills human fears,
Bylgja with her thick mist and eerie fog,
Bara whose foam completes this jotnar epilog.
As we enter your domain, may you clearly see,
We have the utmost respect for your family."

Mr. Young smiles as I finish. "What do you think that means?"

"I don't know," I admit, and everyone else quickly drops their heads in an attempt to avoid getting called on.

That sets Mr. Young up exactly like he wants. He launches into a long discussion about Norse mythology, explaining how the gods and giants behaved. It sounds like they liked to party a bunch, to be honest. I'm not sure that was what I was supposed to get out of this lecture, but nonetheless, that's what I heard.

Apparently, sailors would offer gifts to the sea on each voyage to appease the goddess Ran. They believed that by doing so, Aegir, her husband, and Ran would provide them safe passage.

"So, kind of like a toll tax?" I ask.

Mr. Young nods. "Exactly. They believed that if they didn't pay the tax, they would pay with their lives."

"Sounds a bit dramatic," I say.

"Well, that's Norse mythology for you. It's a wonderful world full of drama, and we're going to be exploring it first this semester. It actually has a lot of similarities to other cultures that may surprise you. Your homework for today is to read the first three chapters and get ready for a quiz tomorrow."

The whole class groans.

As we gather our things, I feel a sense of anticipation. This year is off to an interesting start, and I'm ready to see where it takes us.

As the bell rings, we all make our way to the door as fast as possible to escape any further questioning.

Reading Ahead

Jon

WELL, THAT WAS DIFFERENT. Mr. Young really surprised me with *Jotnar Myths*, but I am glad because I actually read that one as a part of my Bragi studies with Grandpa. That allows me to be on my phone, doing a bit of research into something I want to get more familiar with. But first, I need to catch up with the group that I guided to English to see where they need to go next.

Some of them have study hall, others have gym or choir, but it is clear that only Marc and I need to go to calculus. We do our best to give them directions to where they need to go, and then I motion to Marc that we need to get going.

"I want to stop off at the library really quickly to check out a book that I looked up while I was in English class."

Marc asks, "You were looking up books to read *while* we were reading a book?"

"Yeah. I was looking up books on Skinwalker Ranch in Utah."

"*Utah*? Oh, got it. The place where Sam is from? Yeah, but did you want to talk about what we read today in English? I mean, it was interesting, right?"

"I guess. I have already read that book, though, so I really didn't pay close attention. Besides, we live in Iowa, so a story about gods and goddesses of the sea doesn't seem particularly relevant."

"Obviously. Well, we should probably at least discuss *Jotnar Myths* again with Grandpa."

"That's fine, but first, I definitely want to talk about skinwalkers."

We don't have a lot of time, and I need to get to the library and quickly find this book. I walk in and can instantly smell the books. It's funny how every library basically smells the same, especially if they have older books that have been around for decades, like our school. Some people absolutely hate it and complain about it every time they walk through the door, but I love it and feel right at home.

I make a dash to the front desk computer and type in the book I am after, *Hunt for the Skinwalker*" by George Knapp, and a couple more books that just have snippets on Skinwalker Ranch in Utah. They are buried in the back of the library, but Marc and I split up the list, so we are able to grab them quickly. We then run by a waving Mrs. Snow on the way out the door.

She just says, "Bring them back quick, Jon." She knows me so well that she will let me take any book I want. She's the best.

We barely make it to calculus before Mr. Hildahl starts in with his introductions and another round of meet-your-classmates kicks off. Mr. Hildahl, however, decides that it makes sense to go with two truths and a lie, which immediately tells me this is going to take a while. So, I grab one of the books and lay it behind my calculus book so I can start learning more about skinwalkers to see if anything connects with what I know about Sam.

Apparently, the Myers family, Kenneth and Edith, owned this ranch in Utah for years, and then sold it in the 90s to the Shermans. When the Shermans arrived, they found all kinds of chains, padlocks, bars on the windows, and other items that were intended to secure something. They thought it was strange, but that was nothing compared to the events that started happening to them.

Not long after buying the ranch, they had an encounter with a massive wolf. This wolf casually walked up to them as if it were completely tame. In fact, they even were able to pet this wolf until it snapped its head and ran in the direction of one of their cows. It attacked the cow, and Tom Sherman quickly ran to get his gun. He shot the wolf multiple times, but the wolf was completely fine, as if nothing had happened to it. He repeated this with a shotgun to the same result. This wolf finally got bored and headed off.

The Shermans attempted to track the animal, but after walking for some time, following the wolf's tracks, the tracks just disappeared. They believe that this was their first encounter with a skinwalker.

Skinwalkers are said to have many powers, including incredible speed, strength, and the ability to paralyze people through their touch and through bone powders. At least, that is what the books are saying.

I continue reading, diving deeper into the lore.

Another story that catches my attention involves a family who lived near the ranch in the late 90s. They reported seeing strange animals, including a giant bear-like creature that could run at incredible speeds. One night, the father was outside when he saw the creature and tried to shoot it. The bullet seemed to pass right through it, similar to the wolf. The creature then suddenly vanished, leaving no trace behind.

Another chapter describes an encounter with a skinwalker that paralyzed its victims. A local farmer claimed he was working late one night when he felt a sudden chill and saw a shadowy figure approaching him. Before he could react, the figure touched his shoulder, and he felt a wave of paralysis wash over him. He was unable to move or call for help as the skinwalker rifled through his belongings, seemingly searching for something. It wasn't until the figure left that he regained control of his body.

One of the Navajo legends of skinwalkers is that, to become a skinwalker, there are many dances and songs that need to be learned. In addition, you have to make sacrifices and follow what the "darkness" tells you to do. One thing you must do is kill a loved one in your immediate family—a father, mother, sister, brother, etc.. That is how the process of becoming a skinwalker starts, but it does not end there.

I can't help but draw parallels between skinwalkers and the descendants of Loki. Loki's descendants are tricksters, and forcing someone to kill a loved one sounds like a Loki ploy, somewhat similar to how he tricked Hodor to kill Baldr. Also, Loki was known to be a shapeshifter with the ability to take on any animal form.

I really need to talk with Grandpa to see if my theory has any merit. From what I'm reading, I think it's possible that the "darkness" skinwalkers talk about could be Loki. The thought of that is terrifying, though, because who knows what those creatures could be capable of if that is true?

I snap out of it and look up to see all eyes on me, including Mr. Hildahl. I apologize and say, "I obviously love to read, I am a poet, and I am trying out for football this year."

Before I even finish saying it, Chad Kaiser yells out, "Lie. No way you are playing football, Bragg."

I just nod, as if I'm not completely indifferent, and say, "Yep, you got me. That was the lie." I'm not really trying out, but I didn't need to say what everyone knows.

As soon as I am done and they move on to the next person, I realize I should stop reading for now, pay attention, and wait to talk to Grandpa about all of this tonight.

Mr. Hildahl continues with the introductions, but as we settle into the calculus lesson, my mind keeps wandering back to the stories I just read. The possible connection to Sam and the eerie similarities between the skinwalker legends and Loki's powers are too strong to ignore. I need to find out more, and fast.

After class, Marc and I walk out together.

"That was intense," Marc says, nudging me. "You were really into that book."

"Yeah," I reply, still deep in thought. "There's something about the skinwalkers that's just ... familiar. I think there's a connection to Loki."

Marc raises an eyebrow. "What kind of a connection?"

"I think Loki may have created them. Loki's a shapeshifter, a trickster, and the idea of making someone kill a loved one fits his MO. Sorry, I should tell you that in order to trigger the ability to become a skinwalker, you have to kill someone you love. Sounds like Loki, right? I need to talk to Grandpa about this."

Marc shrugs. "Beats me. I didn't spend the entire hour reading about it, so I'm a little bit behind on this one. You can fill me in tonight when we talk to Grandpa."

As we head to our next class, my mind races, feeling like I am on the verge of uncovering something big. Something that might alter what we thought we knew about magic, myths, and the creatures that walk among us.

Biology

Darla

BY THIRD PERIOD, THE excitement is wearing off, and the grind of being back in school is settling in. Every class has been similar, with the chance to get to know each other better and the propaganda surrounding how great it is that Bluehill and Grinwell combined. I'm not saying it's a bad idea; it's just not something we need to dwell on. It is what it is.

In reality, it's still just school. The only real difference is more kids, more teachers, more noise and, for me, so many more cousins. Unfortunately, I don't have any classes without at least one of them in it this year.

My next class is biology, and my least favorite cousins, Ronny and Gaddy, are in this one with me. So, not only is science—any science—the worst, but I also have to deal with those two.

Sure enough, as soon as I get to class, there are Gaddy and Ronny, motioning me over to sit by them. For whatever reason, I do the opposite and get as far away from them as possible. I just can't … not right now. I can't deal with them.

They look at each other and whisper, no doubt talking about me. I'm sure I'll hear about this later, but I really don't care.

As I am deep in thought, I don't even notice Sam drop into the seat next to me at the lab table.

"What's up, Darla? How's your first day of school going?"

I look up, trying to show I wasn't startled or taken off guard, and just say, "It's school."

Sam nods in agreement. "Yeah, same."

It's good to have Sam because, before I know it, several people from Bluehill surround us. Sam has that effect; everyone who knows him wants to be around him just for his positive energy.

We are in Mr. Fagan's class. He's a skinny man with dark glasses that swallows up his face a little bit. I mean, when you look at him, you only see his glasses. He looks like he could be the smartest person you are ever going to meet.

Before class, he is humming a song and seems completely oblivious to the fact that there is a room behind him, filling up with students. Of course, we all think this is hilarious, and there is already whispering going on. Someone from behind whispers that he looks a bit like a cartoon character. He is prematurely going bald, but you can tell he doesn't care. He wears his confidence well.

When he decides it is time, Mr. Fagan does something shocking. He just starts right into a lecture and skips the routine we all have become too familiar with over the last two periods.

One student toward the front of the class asks, "Mr. Fagan, aren't we going to start by getting to know each other?"

Mr. Fagan just says, "Why? The only thing you need to know is I am your teacher, and this is biology. I'll leave the rest up to you."

Nice. I could have a new favorite teacher. That is, if the subject wasn't biology.

We are told that we are going to do an experiment on the properties of water. The first experiment has to do with cohesion—water molecules sticking to one another. We use a water dropper to drip water onto a penny. We are able to fill the surface of the penny with a dome-like bubble of water. We try it again with really soapy water, and then with rubbing alcohol. So, we have three pennies lined up side by side. We find that the penny with just water has more of a dome than the other two pennies. I guess it has to do with the ability of water to bond with itself. Sam and I agree this is true, and I have to admit it is kind of fun.

"Did you know water has a high surface tension?" Sam asks, his tone curious.

"No, I did not," I reply, looking at our dome-shaped water on the penny.

Sam continues, "It's because of the hydrogen bonds. They're like tiny magnets that hold the water molecules together."

I nod, impressed. "You know your stuff, Sam."

He shrugs. "I like science. Plus, I just heard Mr. Fagan say that to another table."

As we are admiring our work, we notice everyone is gathering around the lab table where Gaddy and Ronny are. When I get over there, I see that Hef has joined them. Even Mr. Fagan is over there, saying, "That is wild. I have never seen that much water collected on a penny."

Hef just keeps dropping water on the penny until the dome is about as high as a penny is wide. It is bizarre.

Gaddy, Ronny, and Hef must think it is hilarious because they just keep giggling. Before I know it, everyone is laughing hysterically, as if this water on the penny is the funniest thing anyone has ever seen. It is weird.

Sam and I just look at each other, shrug, and walk back over to our table.

Gaddy and Ronny shoot a look in our direction that is clearly a look of surprise, and then disdain. Whatever.

The next experiment we do is to pour water into a cup and sprinkle in quite a bit of pepper. Nothing particularly interesting happens until we put a drop of soap in the middle of the mass of pepper. We watch as the pepper spreads away from the soap, sinking and retreating to the edges of the cup. We conclude that because soap is less dense than water, it floats on the surface, acting as a sort of wall atop the water, not mixing in with it because of its cohesive qualities. It pushes the pepper away and down because it is taking up all the surface area on the top of the water.

"That is also kind of cool," I admit.

Mr. Fagan nods. "Yeah, it shows how surface tension works. The soap disrupts the surface tension, causing the pepper to move."

We continue with the experiments, each one demonstrating a different property of water. The next one involves adhesion—water molecules sticking to other surfaces. We dip paper clips into water and watch how they cling to the sides of a glass. The water climbs up the paper clip, defying gravity, showing how adhesion works.

"So, adhesion is like the opposite of cohesion?" I ask.

"Sort of," Mr. Fagan says. "Cohesion is water sticking to water, and adhesion is water sticking to other things."

We then move on to capillary action, where we dip the end of a piece of paper towel into water and watch the water climb up the towel. It is fascinating to see the water move upward against gravity, showing how plants draw water from their roots to their leaves.

"This is how plants get water," Mr. Fagan explains. "The water moves up through tiny tubes in the plant."

"That's surprisingly useful," I say, genuinely intrigued.

Our next experiment involves density. We fill a cup with water and slowly add ice cubes. The ice floats, which we know it will, but it is still interesting to see. Mr. Fagan explains that ice is less dense than liquid water, which is why it floats. We then add salt to the water, and the ice starts to sink as the salt increases the water's density.

We are on our fifth experiment when everyone gathers around Gaddy and Ronny's table again. This time, they are doing the same pepper and soap experiment but with a twist. They have added food coloring to the water, creating a vibrant, swirling effect when the soap hits the water. It is beautiful, but also a bit over the top.

Even Mr. Fagan is impressed. "That's quite a display. You three certainly know how to make an experiment visually interesting."

Gaddy, Ronny, and Hef beam with pride. I guess they like the attention.

Sam leans over and whispers, "They're really into showing off, huh?"

"Always," I reply, rolling my eyes.

The final experiment involves surface tension and buoyancy. We have to float a paperclip on the surface of the water without it sinking. It takes a few tries, but Sam manages to do it. The paperclip floats delicately on the water, supported by the surface tension.

"You've got a steady hand," I say, impressed.

Sam smiles. "Just takes a bit of patience."

As the period is about to end, Mr. Fagan looks up and says, "Hopefully, you all learned some interesting things today about the properties of water. It's my hope that, throughout this year, you will learn about the science behind so much in our world. Today's example is something powerful we take for granted—water. Now, get out of here and have a great rest of your first day here at Grinwell Bluehill High. There, I said it. Cross that off the to-do list."

We gather our things and head out, but not before Gaddy and Ronny shoot me another look. This time, it is more of a challenge. I can tell they aren't going to let my earlier avoidance go unnoticed. Great. Just what I need.

As we leave the classroom, Sam walks with me. "You handled that well, you know."

"What do you mean?"

"If looks could kill, your cousin just committed homicide. What's the deal with you and them?"

I wave it off but appreciate his support. "Thanks, Sam. It's just … complicated."

"I get it. Family always is."

We walk in silence for a moment, the hallways buzzing with the sounds of students moving between classes. I am already starting to dread tonight. My cousins are going to make it even worse with Mother. They are such snitches.

Lunch Mission

Jon

AS I WALK DOWN THE stairs to get to the cafeteria, I can smell
the familiar scents of school food. We have a hot lunch line and a
separate salad bar line. Basically, what that means is if you can't deal
with the Salisbury steak or meat of the day with canned vegetables
and fixings, then you can always count on a fairly decent salad with a
good selection of fruit.

Deep in thought, I take a pass on the hot lunch line and go
straight to the salad bar. I grab as much fresh fruit as I can pile on
my tray and a small square of lettuce with cheese on it. Today, they
also have cottage cheese, so I plop that in a square and throw some
peaches in heavy syrup on top to make the cottage cheese taste better.
It may not be amazing, but it's protein, and I am going to need
something to make it through the rest of the day.

I enter my school code into the system then turn to face the loud
talking and food munching behind me. It looks like several people
made it to the cafeteria before I did.

When it was just Grinwell, there was plenty of seating available,
but it looks like, this year, having a place to sit at lunch is going to
need to be a higher priority.

I scan the room for Marc, knowing he will have saved a spot
for me and, sure enough, there he is, sitting with Jenny, Darla, and
a bunch of her cousins. He starts waving madly, even though I am
pretty sure he knows that I see him.

"Jon, over here," Marc calls out.

I am looking straight at him, and he has a huge smile on his face as he repeats, "Jon, over here," over and over again.

When I get there, he leans his head to the side, motioning toward where I am supposed to sit. Of course, it is right next to Darla. So, I'm between Marc and Darla in a space that is definitely not large enough for me. It is such a tight space that I feel like I have to ask her, "Is it okay if I sit here?"

Darla says, "Sure, Jon. I know Marc was trying his best to make that happen for you."

I can feel myself blushing. "I really didn't know."

She laughs because I know she finds my awkwardness funny. So, I squeeze in as best I can. It's really hard to do because you have nothing to hold onto.

I set my tray down, which basically touches Darla's and Marc's trays on each side, and then I try to maneuver one leg in at a time. Just as I am awkwardly leaning backward, I slip, and my head hits the floor. Not hard enough to do any damage, but hard enough to make a bunch of noise. My feet kick my plate, which ends up turning my plate, bumping Darla's plate, and Marc's plate, too. It is an unfortunate chain of events.

Not long after I hit the ground, Sam is by my side. "Jon, are you okay? How many fingers am I holding up?"

He holds up two fingers, and I say, "Two."

"Cool, let's get you up."

I really don't need help, but I decide to accept it because at least someone is being nice.

As soon as I get up, everyone roars in laughter, and I do the only thing I can do and take a bow. "Thank you. Thank you. I will be appearing daily at this location for your viewing pleasure."

With that, I turn to Marc and Darla and apologize. "I'm so sorry. I didn't mean to."

"I know, Jon," Darla says. "You just can't help it. At least you have a sense of humor about it."

Sam clears some room by him and says, "Why don't you come sit over here? We'll make space."

I pick through the upside-down tray for the fresh fruit, and then take my knife and just slide all the rest off the table, back onto my tray. I won't be eating that, that's for sure.

I get over to where Sam is sitting, and behind him is Brad, of course.

As I get near him, Brad says, "Everyone, hold onto your trays. Bragg is going to try to sit down." Again, not particularly funny, but everybody laughs.

Sam just gives them all a look, and they stop. He motions. "Have a seat, Jon."

I nod a thank you and take a seat in the most uneventful way possible.

I glance over at Marc and mouth, "*I'm sorry.*"

He just shrugs, and I know he is fine.

Darla keeps glancing over at me as if she is checking on me, which amazes me because I would have thought she would be pretty ticked off since I messed up her tray, as well. Why do I always have to do things like that around her? It's getting ridiculous. I'll send her a snap later to apologize, and we'll see if she returns it. I wouldn't blame her if she didn't.

Sam says, "I'd ask you how your day is going, but I think I know."

"Unfortunately, it's a garden-variety day in the life of me. I am kind of accident-prone, if you haven't heard."

"Oh, I remember. Don't worry about it, man. It's not a big deal."

Before I know it, I am deep in the conversation at the table. It is full of Bluehill kids, so I don't know many of them. I guess they don't know me either, but it seems good enough that Sam wants me to sit by him. They are all talking to me as if nothing embarrassing just happened. They are full of questions about the school, to say the least.

They all want to hear the story of Coach Keith and how he was attacked by an animal and killed, and then they want to know about Coach Locke, who seemingly just disappeared. They say there is a bet going around as to whether or not Mr. Sperry will be here next year. They give him at best fifty-fifty odds of returning. I do my best to explain why I think those are isolated incidents. Yet, I get it. It's weird, but if they truly knew how strange the whole thing was, they would be way more concerned about things other than whether or not a teacher would return next year.

I desperately want to ask Sam questions about his family and their past, but I also don't want to push it because he has been a good friend today. I don't want to prod in areas that he might not want to talk about. For now, I decide it is best to just keep an eye on him.

As we wrap up lunch, Sam asks, "Jon, what's your next class?"

"I've got history with Mrs. Kaplan."

"Cool. I'm headed to the same class. We can walk together."

We clear our trays, and as we walk to history class, the conversation turns to the upcoming football season. Sam is excited about trying out for the team, and I can tell he has high hopes of making a difference. He asks me about any sports that I am interested in, and I just say I'm more of a school newspaper type of guy.

History with Mrs. Kaplan is more of the same—introductions and a brief overview of what we'll be covering this year. The highlight is when Mrs. Kaplan mentions how we'll be doing a project on family histories, which gets a few groans from the class but intrigues me. Family history might be a good way to find out more about Sam's ancestors to see if I can piece anything together from that.

After history, I have government with Mr. Preston. He is new to the school, from Bluehill, and it shows. I guess teachers can get nervous, too. The biggest uphill battle for Mr. Preston, though, is going to be keeping everyone awake because of the subject. Government is a required class; otherwise, I am positive nobody would take it.

As the day wears on, I find myself looking forward to the end of the day so I can head home and talk to Grandpa. That last fifteen minutes seems to take an eternity.

As I walk out of the school building, I see Marc waiting for me by the bike racks. He has his usual grin on his face, and I know he is ready to hear all about my theories.

"Hey, Marc," I call out.

"Hey, Jon. Ready to head home?"

"Yeah, let's go. I've got a lot to talk about."

When we get to the Corolla, Jill is already there. I guess that is going to put a damper on the conversation.

"I forgot this morning. Nice parking, loser," she comments.

We are still sandwiched between Brad's car and the monster truck. I guess the football guys are going to practice already.

I decide to let that pass and just say, "Get in." Then I slowly and carefully inch my way out of the spot. I think it takes about ten tries, but I eventually clear both vehicles and we are on our way home, ready for some Bragi training.

The Fight

Darla

THE COUSINS AND I HEAD out to the front of the school to wait for Mother to pick us up. It is a bright, sunny afternoon with clear skies, a perfect day overshadowed by the chaos of the first day of the combined school. Parents are lining up to pick up their kids, creating a maze of cars and confusion. The school staff has someone directing traffic, but it doesn't seem to be helping much. Everyone is trying to figure out the flow, adding to the mess.

One thing about Mother is she is on her own schedule, which is fine because there is a group of us gathering to talk about our day.

I make my way over to Jenny and ask, "Waiting for your parents, too?"

"Yeah, they said it could take a bit today. I guess they both had meetings that could run long. Are you waiting on your dad?"

"I wish. No, we're waiting on Mother," I say.

"Oh yeah, that's right. You said you had something after school, right?" Jenny asks.

"Yeah, can't wait," I reply, dripping as much sarcasm as I can muster into that reply.

"Do you have a lot of homework?"

"Not really. Typical first day."

As Jenny and I talk, I notice Jess has cornered the cousins over by the water fountain and is chatting with them. I point in their direction as I tell Jenny, "I better go see what that's all about."

Jenny says, "Okay, good luck with that. See you tomorrow."

One quick hug, and I say, "See you tomorrow."

As I get closer, I can hear Jess in full-on recruiting mode, trying to convince the cousins to try out for the cheer team. The cousins are filling up their water bottles and sucking down water like they haven't had anything to drink all day. They are so weird.

"Cheerleading tryouts are starting. Coach Handorf says that nobody has a guaranteed spot on the team this year because of the schools merging. So, it's a great opportunity to get involved. It's a lot of fun and a great way to meet more people. Next to the football team, we are probably the most popular squad in school," Jess says.

Gaddy asks, "Is the coach willing to consider other people to be the captain of the team?"

Jess, caught off guard, says, "I guess so. If nobody has a guaranteed spot, that would include me. I'm not worried about that, though."

"Maybe you should be," Gaddy tells her.

Jess has a surprised, deer-in-the-headlights look on her face. It's clear she hasn't really considered that possibility. I am shocked to see this because Jess is always unshakable with the perfect amount of confidence. She doesn't rub it in everyone's face, but we all know she is good and doesn't need us to tell her that. However, Gaddy has gotten to her.

I jump in at that point and say, "Jess, you know you have nothing to worry about. Coach Handorf knows that the whole football team would revolt if you aren't captain again this year. Besides, nobody is as passionate about cheer as you are, and you know it. The whole town knows it."

Jess regains her composure. "That's right. So, as I was saying, you should all try out for the team. We would love to have you." Jess strides away, confidence restored.

With a challenging look on her face, Gaddy says, "Oh, I'll be there."

As soon as Jess walks away, I get in Gaddy's face. "What is your problem?"

"Ha, I don't have any problems, but you do. Why did you blow off Ronny and me today? Mother said you are supposed to take care of us. You ghosted us on purpose."

"Did I? I have no idea what you are talking about."

"Right," Gaddy replies. "We know you saw us in biology, Darla, and we are going to talk to Mother about it."

"Really? That's how this year is going to be? You are going to be a big snitch every day? You know what? Bring it. How much worse could it get?"

"You might be surprised. Why do you hate us so much?"

"Hate you?" I reply. "Why do all of you hate *me* so much?"

Olga jumps into the middle to ease the tension. Immediately, I feel a calming presence and start to relax as she says, "Hey, you two, remember we need each other."

I look back at her and really want so badly to say that I don't *need* any of them. Instead, I say, "I'm sorry, Olga. You are right." It doesn't feel right coming out of my mouth, but I said it, nonetheless.

She continues, "This is new for all of us. We got used to doing our own thing for a long time. While we all accepted coming here, Darla didn't have a say in the matter. We have to remember that. She was already here, and we are guests in her house and in her school. We are sorry, Darla. Right, girls?"

They all nod in agreement, even Gaddy, who at this point is giving Olga a death stare, as well.

I appreciate what she is saying, but I don't really need anyone to fight my battles for me. "Look, I appreciate it, but I'm a big girl, and I can handle whatever the consequences are. I am a Towns, and we never back down from a fight."

"Right. We'll see about that," Gaddy goads.

Just like that, the tension is back in the air, as if it is battling the wave of calm and rolling over it.

Gaddy nods to Ronny then turns to Olga. "We'll talk about this later."

Olga drops her head as if she is in trouble for something.

I get right in Gaddy's face. "You are unbelievable. Olga is just trying to help. Leave her alone."

Gaddy moves forward to shove me, and I use the momentum to throw her over my right hip. She hits the ground hard, but she is up in an instant. The fight is on.

I block her punches and retaliate with a knee strike, followed by a judo throw that sends her sprawling.

We are in a full-on fight now. Everyone who is still at school circles around us, and I can feel hundreds of eyes on us. That only feeds the fire in me, and my training kicks in.

I trained in jiu-jitsu for years with Dad, so I am pretty good. I counter every move and quickly take her back and sink in a rear naked choke with my legs locked around her. I sink it in deeper and deeper. It is clear, though, that Gaddy is not going to tap out. Fine by me.

As she is about to go out, I hear a screaming, "*Darla Bara Towns, you stop that this instant!*"

I release Gaddy, who is gasping for air. She looks back with a grin on her face as if she wanted me to do that. Gaddy then goes to stand over by Mother and pleads with her, "I don't know what has gotten into Darla. We were just talking, and before I knew it, she was choking me."

Mother turns to me, "*In the car—now!* That goes for all of you. We will discuss this in private."

As we make our way to the car, I can feel the stares of everyone around us. I catch a glimpse of Coach Sperry and wonder how much of that he saw.

The bright sun and clear skies do nothing to lighten my mood. Yet, I feel a bit satisfied because it felt really good to best Gaddy. That said, I just want to get away from it all and especially the cousins.

Once we are all in the car, Mother starts driving. The silence in the car is almost deafening. I can feel the tension building, knowing that Mother is going to have a lot to say once we get to wherever we are going. Because of this, the drive feels like an eternity, each minute stretching out as we navigate through traffic and out of town. Where on earth are we going?

Finally, we pull into Harmony Grove of all places. Mother parks the car and turns to face us.

"I don't know what happened today, but Darla, this behavior is unacceptable. We are going to have a long talk about this right here."

We all file out of the car and gather by the lake. Mother's stern expression tells me this is not going to be a pleasant conversation. I brace myself for what's to come, knowing that no matter what, I have to stand my ground.

Totem Pole

Jon

WE DON'T HAVE TOO FAR to go tonight since Marc almost always comes over to our house after school. His parents work in Des Moines, and that's a good ninety minutes from Grinwell. They ride together to save on gas, so that means they have to stay until both of them are done working for the day. That causes them to get home after seven thirty every night, sometimes a little later. We don't mind, though, because it gives us time to study, eat, play games and, of course, now train with Grandpa.

Jill is uncharacteristically quiet for the ride. So much so that I feel I have to ask, "Everything okay, sis?"

"Yeah, it was just a long day. High school is a lot different than junior high. It's rough having to be at the bottom of the totem pole all over again. We just got to the point where we ruled the campus, and now we are back to the bottom. Actually, the top. Our lockers are the farthest away from classes, and I was late to class a couple of times today. I'm going to have to carry extra books to some of the classes tomorrow just to get there on time."

"I get it, but you'll get used to it before you know it. Once you have a routine down, it'll be a piece of cake."

Marc chimes in, "You got this, Jill."

Noticing we are all having a moment, she then blurts out, "Plus, my brother spazzed out today and fell on his butt in front of the whole school at lunch. So, all afternoon, I got to hear about that from everyone I met. Any suggestions on how to deal with that, losers?"

I just reply, "Yeah, I love you, too, sis."

Which earns me a hand to the back of my head after which she drops her eyes back to her phone and starts typing away. No doubt something touching to say about us to her friends.

I do kind of feel for her. Marc and I know what it's like to be at the bottom of the school social totem pole. In fact, we frequently feel like we are still there. It's super important, though, to keep everything in perspective.

As a descendant of Bragi, I could use my powers in so many different ways to help her, but the reality is, it's good that she is going through this right now. It's important to have some challenges, as it develops the ability to overcome them. Also, I know good and well that we aren't supposed to draw attention to ourselves by using our powers. It could easily be noticed and cause the APS to have to take action, or it might bring other worse things our way. Yep, the school social scene is just something everyone has to endure.

With that, we are home, and Jill gets out of the car as fast as possible, as if spending one more second with Marc and me would kill her.

Marc and I walk in the front door, grab a snack from the kitchen, and then make our way down to the basement to talk with Grandpa.

Ever since Grandpa got really sick due to Coach Locke draining his blue essence—our source of power—he has lived with us. At first, he stayed in my room, but my parents finished the basement and turned it into an apartment. Now, Grandpa stays down there, which is perfect because it is a great place for us to do our Bragi training and keeps him close so I can ask questions and learn from him.

Grandpa is clearly setting up for training, but first, Marc and I jump at the chance to fill him in on what we learned today.

I start first, asking, "Grandpa, what do you know about skinwalkers?"

"Hey, Jon, how was your day?"

I realize that I skipped the usual pleasantries. "Sorry, Grandpa. My day was decent. I only had the whole school laughing at me once. How was your day?"

"So far so good."

For as long as I have known him, that has always been his answer to anyone who ever asks how he is doing. He says that because, as he says, "Your day can turn on a dime at any moment," so he prefers to state that everything is going okay, at least to the best of his knowledge. Even though we always know what his answer will be, it's still polite to ask.

Feeling satisfied, Grandpa responds, "Skinwalkers have been talked about for ages. The last I knew, they were isolated to the mountains in the Northwest. I suppose it's possible for them to be elsewhere, but they tend to stay close to their tribe and to the land where they were born and are connected to."

"I read up some on them today, and I was wondering if they were created by a descendant of Loki. They have quite a few powers that are similar to his, and the books mention a darkness that just reminds me of the darkness that surrounded Coach Locke."

"That's very observant, Jon. As a matter of fact, most of the creatures you hear about were created by a descendant of Asgard. That includes vampires, witches, and werewolves, which share a very similar magic to skinwalkers."

That catches Marc and I off guard a bit but also makes so much sense. I now have a bunch of additional questions about all of those creatures, but those will have to wait. *Focus, Jon, focus.*

Grandpa goes on to describe that legend has it that the Navajo tribe in and around Utah had the ability to take the shape of animals that was gifted to them by Odin himself from the beginning.

However, Odin made it incredibly difficult for them. They had to learn a large number of dances and songs in order to be able to transform themselves. "Similar to how we train you for your Bragi skills. They were deeply personal, like your rhymes, and some in the tribe spent years and years of their lives trying to learn how to transform."

One day, a descendant of Loki crossed their paths and told them there was a shortcut they could take to become a skinwalker. Being ever the trickster, he didn't tell them everything they would have to do. Instead of memorizing dances and songs, he had them carry out sacrificial rituals, including murdering loved ones. Of course, that wasn't really necessary; Loki just wanted to see what they would do to get power, and the answer was frightening, but not surprising. They would do anything.

"The APS has a special unit that hunts down any skinwalkers with the goal of determining if they come from Odin's line of skinwalkers or Loki's. If they come from Odin's line, they are left alone because they have earned the right to their powers through noble means. However, if they come from Loki's line, they have to be detained, or worse, if they fought justice—they have to be incarcerated or taken care of by other means.

"Why are you interested in skinwalkers, Jon?"

"Because one of the guys from scout camp goes to our school now. It's Sam, the one I told you about. It turns out he moved to Bluehill in sixth grade, and prior to that, he lived around where Skinwalker Ranch lies in Utah and went to the school on the reservation there."

"Oh, I see. You are wondering if his DNA might register as a giant. It might. I'm not sure about that. I'll have to ask the APS to look into that and let us know. In the meantime, why don't you just keep an eye on Sam. Remember, if he does come from a line of skinwalkers, be careful. You don't know which type of skinwalker he might be. We also don't know if he really is one or not. Let's not jump to conclusions."

Marc then asks Grandpa about the *Jotnar Myths* from today's English class.

Grandpa thinks it's quite an interesting choice for a high school English class and says, "I wonder why he decided to use that book."

"In class, Mr. Young talked about studying diverse cultures and learning from them," Marc replies.

"Sure, that sounds like a good idea, but why a book about Norse culture? How many people in Grinwell, or Bluehill, are there who could possibly relate to that? That's the part of this that I find peculiar. What on earth put him up to studying that text? It's obscure, at best." Grandpa then shrugs it off. "All right, enough of that. I have something special for today's training session."

Marc and I look at each other, curious and excited. Grandpa rarely mentions having something special for training, so this piques our interest.

"What's the special training, Grandpa?" Marc asks.

Grandpa smiles, a twinkle in his eye. "Patience, boys. First, let's warm up with our usual routine. We need to be ready for anything."

We start out with our usual exercises, which involve rhymes to manipulate the elements. Then Grandpa turns in the *Book of Bragi* to protection spells.

The Lake

Darla

AS SOON AS I STEP ONTO the beach at Harmony Grove, a flood of emotions hits me. The water in the air feels almost electric, amplifying my feelings until it's almost overwhelming. Fear, anger, happiness, and every other emotion I have ever felt surge through me all at once. I have to catch my breath. I have never felt anything like this before. I guess I'm just anxious about what Mother is going to do. I don't know, but I don't like it.

Flashbacks from scout camp with Jon bombard my mind. We did so much together, and while it was his fault that I was captured by Coach Locke, he was also the one who came to save me. He put himself in harm's way when he didn't have to, just to come and rescue me. He could have run, but he didn't. I can still feel him next to me, sitting by the lake the night before I was taken. He gets me, certainly more than Mother and these cousins do.

Mother snaps, "Darla! Pay attention! You need to grow up and start behaving like the giant you are."

"This is stupid," I mutter.

"Oh, *this* is stupid? Is that what you think? I'll tell you what is stupid. It's idiotic that someone as powerful as you is acting like this. You are so ungrateful. Do you know how hard it was to assemble all of you? I spent all my days while your father was in the field online, searching for each of your cousins. There were so many dead

89

ends and fools trying to lie to me. And now I need *all* of you. That includes you, Darla Bara. It's time you get with the program.

"Gaddy, would you mind taking the lead on this one? Girls, I want you to gather around Bara, holding hands."

"No, thanks. Not interested, Mother."

Then something happens. Mother's voice booms in my head.

"*Shut up, Bara! Stand still!*"

It's like she has a microphone, and her voice is amplified. It rattles around in my head.

Is there an echo here at Harmony Grove? How did that happen?

Suddenly, I am struck by the inability to move and the inability to talk. I can see everything that is happening, though.

She has my attention now as fear starts building up inside of me.

My cousins gather around me, holding hands. I look from face to face, trying to get a reaction, but all I get is excited smiles flashing back at me. They are enjoying whatever is about to happen, that is clear.

The water starts rising from its banks, approaching us. It's creeping toward us slowly at first, and then accelerating as if it just broke free from a dam. Then it carries me into the middle of the lake.

I say "it" as if the water has a mind of its own, but at this point, I have no idea what is happening. I am completely submerged and cannot breathe. I start to panic and try my best to kick and fight this, but it's no use.

Just as I think I cannot hold my breath any longer and start to think about everyone I love—my dad, Jenny, and Jess—we go deeper and deeper until I think something is wrong. We should have reached the bottom by now.

Something then literally pops in my head as I see us pass through some sort of entrance, and then I can breathe.

Am I below the water now? I see some kind of walls, and I'm still in the middle of everyone. They are all looking down at me, but everything is still spinning out of control.

I notice the underwater world around me. It's eerie and beautiful, like something out of a fantasy movie. The water is different, shallow at my knees, and blue like the ocean instead of the previous muddy brown lake water, and I can see strange, glowing plants swaying gently in the current. Small, luminescent fish dart past, their scales shimmering like rainbows. It's mesmerizing, and for a moment, I forget my fear.

I see schools of tiny fish swimming together in perfect harmony, their movements synchronized as if they are performing a dance just for me. The plants on the walls seem to shine with an inner light, casting a glow on everything around them.

"What just happened? What are you doing to me? Where are we?" I struggle to try to get to my feet, but the world around me starts to spin. I try to ask for help. "Mother, I don't feel well." Then I feel myself falling backward as the world around me fades, an all-too-familiar feeling as I am consumed by the darkness.

I WAKE UP IN THE TAHOE, wrapped in a blanket. Suddenly, I can hear all of my cousins talking to me and waking me up.

As I open my eyes, I can still hear them, but they aren't talking with their mouths. They are congratulating me on becoming one of them ... *in my head*!

What are they talking about? I *almost* died.

Right?

Olga's thoughts come rushing in, "*We would never let anything happen to you, sister.*"

I think something is terribly wrong with me right now. I am absolutely hearing things.

As we pull into the driveway at home, Mother turns and looks straight at me. "Not a word to anyone about this! *Including* your father!"

Immediately, I say, "Yes, Mother."

I have never been more terrified of her in my life. What she did was unimaginable. I could have died. Or did I? What happened exactly?

"We will talk more about this tomorrow after school. Get some rest. I'll have the girls bring up a tray of food for you later," Mother says. "Girls, help her to her room before her father gets home."

When Olga brings up my dinner, I am exhausted but decide to ask her some questions.

"What actually just happened, Olga?"

"You became one of us today. Well, you already were one of us; you just needed a bit of a push to fully trigger everything. You know, your powers. It was Mother's idea."

"But I could have died. And what powers? I don't feel any different, and I definitely don't feel powerful in any way. I feel anything but powerful. I feel violated!"

"We wouldn't have let you die, silly. We were right there the whole time."

"Are you sure? Because I am not so sure."

"Darla, I need to get back to the others before Mother gets upset. You should eat and then get some rest. I promise this will all make sense soon. We all went through something similar. It's no big deal. Just relax."

Something about Olga has a way of calming me down. Despite what just happened, I somehow know it is going to be okay.

I eat, change into pajamas, and slide into bed. Homework, what little there is, will have to wait. I need to rest, to relax.

I wake up several times because I keep having nightmares about drowning. It happens over and over again, as if I am replaying it on a loop. It is equally scary each time until I eventually realize I can breathe. I don't mean come up for air every minute or so. I mean, I can breathe, like I am standing on dry land. Surely, that must have been a dream. That can't be real, right? Because that would mean that we somehow were able to just walk right through the bottom of the lake and there was something below it.

My mind also keeps flashing back to all the feelings that I felt on the lake. So many feelings. I swear I could feel what the fish were feeling, the turtles, the frogs, and everyone near the water. It was an overwhelming moment. I felt fish that were lost from their mother because something pulled her out of the lake today when she'd been searching for food. I felt love as if some had found their mates. I felt envy from my cousins that Mother was actually my mother. I don't know what they are jealous about because Mother just about got me killed tonight!

Every time I am about to drown in my nightmares, I remember Dad being there. He is as big and as loving as ever, saying, "Darlin', everything is going to be okay. I'm with you, and I'll protect you." I also think of Jenny and how much she cares about me, and then I think of Jon. Every time I imagine being held in his arms, a pop happens, and I can breathe. I try to stand up, and then I pass out, waking up only to relive it again upon returning to sleep. This happens over and over throughout the night. Needless to say, it is a long night.

As I lie there, exhausted after unsuccessfully trying to make sense of everything, I remember the poem we read in English class and one part comes to mind.

"Keep Ran calm and under your firm control lest she lure us all in her fatal thrall and drags us with her net to depths below where we will be lost forever as you know."

These lines about Ran dragging sailors to their death make me think about what happened to me. Did they die or did they go somewhere else?

As the first light of dawn breaks through my window, I manage to fall into a deeper sleep. The nightmares seem to have subsided, replaced by a sense of calm. Whatever the day ahead holds, I know I need to face it head-on. I am Darla Bara Towns, and I won't let fear control me. After all, it's just an emotion.

The Workout

Jon

I GOT AROUND EARLY this morning because, for whatever reason, I agreed to meet Sam and Taylor at school to work out. They are both trying out for the football team, and I am just interested in keeping an eye on Sam. It's too perfect an opportunity to pass up. If he is a skinwalker, it may be easier to tell in the gym than anywhere else.

Last night, after manipulating air to blow out some candles, which is one of our Bragi warm-up drills, we got to the main event that Grandpa had planned with the APS. He asked the team there to have the descendants of three different gods or goddesses put a protection spell on three different eggs. Then we turned to the base rhymes in the *Book of Bragi*, which went through the steps to break a protection spell.

The first step is to verify that a protection spell is in place. To do that, Marc and I had quite a bit of fun tossing the eggs back and forth. We even dropped them a few times, and nothing happened to them. It was pretty crazy to see how effective the protection spells were. Of course, Grandpa had some fun, too, because he put them in a carton full of eggs. So, Marc and I made quite a mess as only three of the eggs were protected.

After getting nine eggs on our hands and clothes, we finally focused on the three eggs that were protected. The next step is to try to determine which god or goddess is responsible for the protection spell. To do that, I needed to create a rhyme that genuinely requested the egg to identify its protector.

> "As I see that you have been made secure,
> Please identify so I can know for sure,
> Which god from Asgard has made you so,
> You will be safe from every single foe."

As I worked on the rhymes, I realized that if I asked with sincerity and made it known to the egg that I was Bragi, it would let its guard down enough to reveal to me who protected it. One of the eggs was protected by a descendant of Thor, another was protected by a descendant of Heimdall, and one was protected by a descendant of Odin himself.

After identifying the god, according to the *Book of Bragi*, it is required to make a plea to that god to remove the protection spell. It also says that the length and detail of the plea are dependent on how large the protection spell appears to be. Since this was just an egg, I determined that the spell would be short. It cannot take much power to protect an egg. Which, by the way, is something I definitely want to explore next myself.

> "Thank you for identifying for me once before,
> That you were protected by a descendant of Thor.
> Now I ask that you grant me this one request,
> To give up your safety so I can pass this test."

In this manner, I proceeded to remove the protection spells created by Thor and Heimdall relatively quickly, but the protection spell from Odin was different. It was more powerful and resisted removal. No matter what rhyme I tried, I was unable to remove that protection spell, which is exactly what Grandpa knew would happen. Any spells from Odin take more than just words to break. Odin requests a greater show of a strong emotion to grant the release of the protection spell. I tried everything, but that spell remained in place, and that egg was saved from becoming an omelet for another day. Grandpa told me to think about that one as my homework.

After we cleaned up from the training exercise, we enjoyed a wonderful breakfast-for-dinner with my family. Each of us talked about our day and how it went at school. I could tell Mom had already talked with Jill because Jill was far more positive with her outlook than she had been earlier in the car. Mom is so good at allowing you to see clearly that you are making a big deal out of nothing most of the time.

I told them I was most excited about English because we were going to explore different cultures this semester, and I mentioned that Mr. Young even dressed up today—well, he wore a helmet. Dad thought that was funny and placed his hands up on the side of his head with his pointer fingers sticking out of each side. "I don't want to toot my own horns, but today was a good day at work, as well." Apparently, Dad solved some major technology problem for his company today. None of us really understood what he was talking about, but we did our best to humor him. I'm sure he does the same for us most nights. That's what families do—we listen to whatever is important to each other.

It was an all-around good night. Then I took Marc home and reminded him that I would swing by bright and early in the morning to hit the gym. Jill was actually in agreement with going to school early because she wanted to get to the old gym to prepare for cheer tryouts. Since she is in dance and knows Jess really well, she is hoping to make the cheer team this year, which is not going to be easy for a freshman. She told us last night that she heard there were going to be double the girls trying out but only the same number as last year would make the team. It's not going to be easy, so she wants to practice her gymnastics before school. So that was settled.

We get up early enough that this morning is going to have to be the breakfast of champions. I woof down two bowls of Wheaties and a glass of milk as Jill watches impatiently, waiting for me to finish. Of course, that makes me fake another bowl of cereal, to which she says, "Seriously? You are such a pig."

I snort as loudly as I can as I put the bowl in the dishwasher and the cereal back in the pantry. Then I proceed to tell her how intelligent pigs are, so, "Thank you for the compliment."

The Corolla has been acting up a bit lately, and today is no exception. It groans and groans before finally starting, which reminds me that I need to tell Mom and Dad about that. For whatever reason, I always forget about it as soon as I get inside the house. It's like magic. I guess, out of sight, out of mind. Thankfully, it starts up, and we are on our way, off to explore the wonderful world of early mornings at school.

By the time Marc and I get into the locker room, Sam and Taylor are already there.

Sam says, "Ready to hit the weight room?"

"Of course, as long as it isn't leg day."

"Every day should be leg day," Sam says, "but let's see what's available."

I groan, but we all make our way to the weight room, nonetheless.

When we get there, it is packed. This is another downside to the schools merging. There are just way more of us trying to use everything. The Grinwell football team is all present, it seems, led by their fearless leader, Brad.

As soon as we walk into the room, Brad makes his way over to Sam and asks if he wants to hop in with the team.

"Sure," Sam says, "we would all be happy to work out with you."

"Well, we lift fairly heavy. Maybe Bragg better sit this one out," Brad says.

Of course, Brad has no idea what I can do as a descendant of Bragi, which is perfect because I have no intention of showing him or anyone else.

Marc jumps in and says, "Yeah, I bet Jon can lift more than you."

I quickly say, "No way. I'm happy to sit this one out. Not a problem, guys."

Perfect, I now have an excuse to just observe how they do. Of course, this is a weight room full of testosterone, so the only place that they can go first is the bench press area. There are two benches, and the team is sitting down two at a time as they put on more and more weight. They are having a bit of a competition to see how much each of them can bench.

Taylor is pretty quickly out of the competition, but he manages to lift one hundred seventy-five pounds, which is more than I would have thought. Sam and the starting team keep going, blasting through two hundred twenty-five and on their way up to three hundred fifteen. When they get to that, it is only Sam and our biggest linebacker, Myron Wendell, left. Sam knocks out two clean reps, but Myron needs help to get that weight off his chest, making Sam the winner and no doubt the talk of the school soon.

Everyone takes turns smacking Sam on the shoulder to congratulate him. It is a good show of strength, but is it something that requires more than human strength? I can't say that, because Myron is right there with him. For now, the results are inconclusive. I'm going to need to collect more data.

That takes way longer than anyone expected, and we run out of time to do anything else. That works out for me because I got everything I wanted out of this morning's exercise. We all retreat to the locker room to get ready for school. Thankfully, no need to shower, so Marc and I get out of there first and head to class.

The Command

Darla

THIS MORNING, INSTEAD of playing the usual game of trying to get some bathroom time to get ready, I decided to play my other favorite game, which is to avoid everyone I possibly can—except Dad.

I head out to the barn to do some chores and, really, to just get away from the noise of the house. It's a crisp morning with a touch of a chill in the air, announcing that fall is coming. But it will warm up today to reach a comfortable eighty degrees by mid-afternoon. In other words, it's a perfect day to see a sunrise and just be grateful to be alive, especially after whatever happened last night.

I am still feeding the chickens and cleaning their coop when Dad comes up from behind and surprises me with a soft, "Mornin', darlin'. It's a beautiful day, isn't it?"

I just nod.

"Oh, cat got your tongue?" That always brings a smile to my face, and it is always accompanied by Dad meowing like a cat. Although, when he does it, it sounds much longer and exaggerated, but his voice is so high it always makes me laugh.

"No, good morning, Dad. I'm just deep in thought."

"Well, there's no better way to do some thinkin' than a bit of manual labor. What's on your mind, darlin'?"

I pause, and then I decide to say, "I got into it with Gaddy yesterday, and Mother was really upset. She didn't even want to hear what happened."

"Go on. You've got my attention."

"Well, Gaddy was being really rude to Jess, and I know she was doing it on purpose. So, I asked her what her problem was, and before I knew it, we were on the ground, and I was choking her. Mother came right then, and she got *really* mad."

"I see. darlin', you know that was wrong, right? No matter what happens, you should always solve problems with words before resorting to violence."

"I know, Dad, but it's just so hard with them. I feel like Mother actually loves them more than she loves me."

"Oh, kiddo, your mother has trouble expressing her emotions, you know that. She loves you more than anything in this world, and that's something that I know for a fact. She would do anything for you, darlin'."

"Well, she has a funny way of showing it."

"Did something else happen?"

I'm about to tell him about the lake, but honestly, I'm still not sure if that was a nightmare of some sort. I'm not ready to talk about that. Not even with Dad. But before I have a chance, I hear Mother yell, "Darla, hurry up! You're going to be late!"

"Speak of the devil," I say.

Dad just shakes his head and, with a warm smile, says, "Have a good day, darlin'."

I grab the eggs from the coop and bring them into Mother.

"Don't dally around in the mornings, Darla. Your cousins need to eat, and we need the eggs earlier."

"Yes, Mother."

"Now, go get cleaned up and ready for school."

"Yes, Mother."

With that, my quiet start to the day ends, and I join the fray, fighting to get a shower and a bit of mirror time from my cousins, all while doing my best to avoid Gaddy. I just can't deal with her right now.

I can't be happier to get out of the house and off to school, especially given that I'm going to get to drive today since Mother isn't coming. However, as soon as I get out to the Tahoe, I see that Gaddy has plopped herself behind the wheel.

"I don't think so. I'm driving today," I tell her.

Gaddy then does something strange. She yells a demand, and I swear she does it without even opening her mouth, that I stop and listen. Suddenly, I can't move.

I start shaking a bit as I try to fight back from whatever is happening to me. Am I sick? Is she talking? What in the world is going on?

Then I hear Gaddy's voice again, demanding that I shut up and get in the back seat like a "good little girl." The way that is said is so patronizing, but I can't stop my body from first nodding my head and then involuntarily making my way to grab what little room is left in the back seat.

Gaddy looks up in the rearview mirror with a smug grin on her face and says out loud, "That's better, sis."

Wonderful, is this how it is going to be now? Am I suddenly a puppet to be manipulated by Gaddy and my cousins? I am furious, scared, anxious, and every other emotion all jumbled together. Mostly, I just want whatever is happening to stop.

Olga slides her arm around me in a side hug and says, "It's okay. It will get better, Darla. You'll see."

As soon as we get to school and meet up with Jess, we hear the latest gossip. Apparently, Sam won some sort of lift-off this morning that has everyone talking about how strong he is. Of course, I already know that.

"Sam has always been the strongest person in school, ever since junior high. Well, in Bluehill at least," I say.

The cousins, especially Gaddy, are all too interested in learning more about Sam. I have to say something.

"Leave him alone. He's a good guy and one of my best friends."

Gaddy says, "Oh, perfect then. I'll have to pay him a little visit today."

Then I hear her voice again inside my head. "*I will do what I want with whomever I want until* you *start working with us.*"

I look around to see if anyone else heard that. Then I look at Jess, who is busy chatting away. I look at the other cousins, but they just look away. I don't even know what that means. What I do know is that I have no intention of doing *anything* that Gaddy wants me to do.

"Whatever. I'm out of here." I head to find Jenny or anyone whom I can talk to. Then I head straight for my locker, and as I get up the stairs and turn the corner onto our floor, I run smack-dab into Jon and nearly fall back toward the stairs. I reach for him, and Jon catches me. Once my balance is restored, I can't help but pull him in closer and drop my head on his shoulder.

"Sorry, Darla, I didn't see you coming."

I don't say anything. I just stay in the embrace, probably for a bit too long. Jon doesn't seem to mind. Then he helps me walk toward my locker, and we stand there for a minute. I have my head down and am deep in thought, caught in another whirlwind of emotions.

"Is everything okay, Darla?" Jon asks.

I just shake my head. "No, not really."

"Do you want to talk about it?"

"No, not really."

"Okay, well, if you change your mind, just let me know. I'm glad I ran into you this morning. It's really good to see you. I've missed you since camp."

With that, my confusion suddenly clears up, and I just say, "I missed you, too, Jon."

As we stand there, the bustle of the school morning rushes around us. Students chatter and laugh, lockers slam, and the hum of activity fills the air. The sunlight streaming through the windows casts a warm glow on the hallway, a stark contrast to the chill in my heart. The Tahoe ride and my confrontation with Gaddy still bother me, but Jon's presence is calming my nerves.

Jon shifts his weight and looks around the busy hallway. "Hey, if you want, we can find a quiet spot to talk. Sometimes it helps, you know?"

I nod, appreciating his concern. "Yeah, maybe later. I just need to get through the morning right now."

He smiles, a reassuring gesture that makes me feel a bit lighter. "All right, but don't forget I'm here. We've been through a lot together, Darla. You don't have to handle everything on your own."

"Thanks, Jon."

Jon walks me to my first class, and even though we are just walking in silence, it feels so much better.

Jon's a good guy. I know he knows a lot about all of this stuff, but I'm just not ready to talk to anyone. I'm not even sure what is going on right now. Maybe my cousins are just driving me crazy. I have to get this sorted out. I'm sure this is going to occupy my daydreaming in classes today. I've always wondered: when it's more of a nightmare, do you still call it daydreaming? I need to find Jenny as soon as I can, although I'm not sure what I'll even tell her.

Messy Pants

Jon

I WONDER WHAT IS BOTHERING Darla. I can tell as soon as I see her that something is weighing heavily on her. I can't believe I almost ran her over again. I'm just so lucky that she didn't fall backward or break anything.

Speaking of breaking things, I brought the remaining unbreakable egg with me today. Grandpa says I should keep it with me to see if I can sense when or if it is open to a spell to drop its protection. Something about it does feel different.

I pop into the restroom and take a quick scan of my surroundings. The tiled floor is slightly damp, and the fluorescent lights flicker intermittently, casting a faint, uneven glow. The air smells faintly of bleach and cheap air freshener, which could be worse.

I walk down the row of stalls, pushing each door open to make sure they're empty. Satisfied that I'm alone, I then head to the farthest stall for added privacy. I lean in close to the stall door, keeping my voice barely above a whisper and speaking rapidly as I say:

> "I call on you, Odin, to listen to me,
> As somehow I can already tell,
> that you are now open to help me,
> ready to release your safety spell."

Someone charges into the bathroom, slamming the door against the wall. Great, it's Brad.

I drop the egg in my pocket and collect my books in a rush to leave.

As I take a step to pass him, he bumps into me hard and says, "Oops." I fall into the sink, and the worst-case scenario happens—the egg gets smashed. Even more unfortunately, Brad hears the egg crack, and he definitely sees the result. He immediately starts pointing and laughing.

"Geesh, Bragg, check your pants."

I head straight into a stall, drop my books on the shelf, and start cleaning. Meanwhile, I listen to Brad.

"Wait until everyone hears about this. Ha, that's a new one, even for you, Bragg."

As Brad hurries out to no doubt tell everyone about what happened, he shouts, "Bye, Jonboy, see you in the hall."

Sometimes, I really have to fight against wanting to use my powers. I know he's just a stupid bully and not worth it, but sometimes, I think it would feel so good to just smack him on the nose or give him a black eye. But that's not the answer. Instead, I decide to just clean up this mess.

"Make the mess I see in my pants,
dry up and then disappear.
Make them appear as good as new,
before I walk out of here."

With that, my pants are clean, and I do my best to be calm and collected as I walk out of the bathroom and face the waiting crowd.

As soon as I get out, Brad, his football buddies, and Sam are standing outside the bathroom. I have my books down, covering where the stain would be.

Brad points and laughs. "Move the books, Bragg."

"No, that's okay. I have to get to class."

Brad and the team block my movement forward.

"Move the books, Bragg, or I'll move them for you."

"Geesh, okay, Brad, no problem."

Brad points at my pants as a reflex and looks at everyone. However, none of them are reacting as he expects. They are just looking at him and shrugging. He takes a look then does a double-take before scratching his head as if he doesn't get what happened.

"What the heck? How did you do that, Bragg?"

"What is your problem, Dillon?" Sam asks. "There's nothing on his pants. Just leave Jon alone already. I'm already getting tired of your stupid games. Let's go, Jon."

With that, everyone backs off, and Sam and I head down the hall.

Brad calls out, "I know what I saw. I'll see you later, Bragg."

I just reply, "Not if I see you first."

Everyone laughs at that.

I don't turn around to look, but I'm sure Brad doesn't care for that. Yeah, that was better than giving him a bloody nose or black eye. Way better.

"What is his problem with you?" Sam asks.

"I don't know. I guess it's because he knows I used to have a thing for Jess. I mean, for years. I'm over that now, but I don't think he is for some reason. It's dumb."

"Some people just can't leave well enough alone. They have to try to make themselves feel bigger by putting other people down. I really hate bullies; it's not okay. I'm sorry you have to go through that, Jon."

"It's really not a big deal. I truly don't care. It doesn't get to me as much as he thinks it does."

"Well, maybe it doesn't bother you, but it definitely bothers me. I am going to find a way to put a stop to it. That's for sure."

"Don't worry about it, Sam. Really, it's not a big deal. He's not worth it."

I point to indicate this is my class, and he gives me a fist-bump then heads down the hall toward his next class.

Whether or not Sam is a skinwalker, he's definitely a stand-up guy. He's also going to be a solid person to hide behind. With him around, I won't have to use my powers to keep Brad or anyone else in check.

Sam is clearly not going to put up with any bullying around him. Boy, I could have used having him around before becoming a Bragi. Then again, maybe I wouldn't appreciate being a Bragi as much if I didn't go through all of my experiences up to that point.

As I walk into home economics, I'm immediately hit with the scent of vanilla. It's a small classroom, with bright posters of food pyramids and cooking techniques covering the walls. The tables are arranged in a way that makes it look more like a mini kitchen than a typical classroom. I see Jenny and Jess already seated at one of the tables, giggling over something.

"Hey, Jon. Over here." Jess waves at me, pointing to an empty seat next to her.

I make my way over and sit down, feeling slightly out of place among all the girls. Home economics isn't exactly my first choice, but it's an elective that fits into my schedule, and I figured it might be useful to learn some cooking skills this year.

"I heard what happened with Brad," Jenny says, assuming I may be upset.

I sigh. "It's amazing how fast word spreads around here, but yeah, he's just being himself. Nothing new."

Jess rolls her eyes. "I tell him every day that he needs to grow up. Sometimes, he drives me crazy, but he's not always like that, Jon. He just seems to get like that around the team. Anyway, today, we're baking cookies. I hope you're ready to get your hands dirty."

"Cookies, huh? I can handle that." I try to sound more confident than I feel. I also don't want to get into a conversation about Brad with Jess. That could only make the situation worse.

Mrs. Dunham, our home economics teacher, claps her hands to get everyone's attention. She's a cheerful woman, in her early forties, with a perpetual smile that says she is confident and happy but also don't mess with her. Honestly, she scares me a little. Maybe it's the subject that is intimidating because I actually have to do stuff instead of just reading and reciting what I have learned.

"All right, class, today, we're going to learn how to bake chocolate chip cookies from scratch. Team up and gather your ingredients from the pantry. Remember, teamwork is key."

Jess and Jenny immediately start gathering ingredients, and I follow their lead. Flour, sugar, butter, eggs, vanilla extract and, of course, chocolate chips. We bring everything back to our table and start measuring out the ingredients.

As we work, Jess keeps the conversation lively. "So, Jon, do you bake often?"

"Not really," I admit. "This is kind of new for me. Mom does all of this for us."

"Well, maybe you can help her out the next time. You know moms like to be cooked for, too, right?" Jenny says.

"That's a really good idea, Jenny. We definitely take her for granted. I would love to do something nice for her like that." I really believe that, but I also realistically know that I am probably not going to actually do it. I should, but I probably won't.

We mix the ingredients, following Mrs. Dunham's instructions. The kitchen fills with the sound of laughter and the clatter of mixing bowls. It's actually kind of fun, working with Jess and Jenny. Maybe I am going to enjoy this class after all.

Swimming Pool

Darla

EVERY CLASS STARTED off well today. I'm interested in them—I really am—but today, I am struggling to care and to pay attention. No matter how hard I try, it is impossible to make it through a class without drifting into daydreams or whatever you're supposed to call these distractions while the teacher is talking. It's what happened after school yesterday.

Did Mother intentionally drown me? What actually happened? I can't exactly remember. All I know is, one minute, I was on the beach in the middle of a circle, and the next, I was under water and struggling for my life. Until I wasn't. I broke free of the water and then somehow got to shore. Is that right?

The more I think about it, the more jumbled up it's getting in my brain.

Also, what happened today in the Tahoe. Did Gaddy control me? Did that really happen? I am positive that whatever is going on with Mother and the cousins is something I am not interested in *at all*. There is no way that it seems to be a positive for me, no matter how I look at it.

That said, who can I talk to about this? I can't talk to Jenny or Jess. They are just going to think I am crazy. I could talk to Jon, but is that a smart thing to do? If this is really happening, what would that mean to him? Would he have to do something about it? Would people come sweeping in like they did at scout camp to wipe out memories? It's too risky. I am going to have to figure this out on my own.

Lunch is uneventful. Everyone has already figured out that they need to quickly head to the cafeteria if they want to have any say in where they sit. There are just so many of us here that space is a rare commodity, and those who get there early control it.

Without having to say anything, we seem to have mostly separated into tables of Bluehill versus Grinwell students. There are a few exceptions. Sam seems to have taken to Jon, and that means Marc, too, so they crossed school lines and sit with us at a Bluehill table. I don't mind at all.

The conversation is mostly about school and which teachers have already started piling up on the homework. Then it breaks into lots of individual conversations as the noise level in the cafeteria goes from a dull thunder to a loud roar. It's great for avoiding conversation, which is exactly what I am trying to do with Jenny.

Jenny prompts, "So, what happened yesterday after school?"

"Oh, it was really nothing. I just got into it with Gaddy over how she was treating Jess."

"Not that, Darla. I get that. What happened after that? Didn't you have something with your mother and cousins?"

"Well, honestly, I would just like to forget about that. Is that okay?"

"Oh, that bad, huh? Yeah, sure, I'll drop it, but only if you tell me about what happened with Jon this morning. Stacy said she saw you and him together when she got to her locker this morning."

"Yeah, long story short: I ran into Jon at the top of the stairs and almost fell backward, but Jon caught me. Then we were just talking."

"Well, it sounded like more from what Stacy said."

"Jon's a good guy and has a lot going for him. I have been snapping with him since scout camp. We went through a lot together there. You know, we were paired up a lot."

"So, are you two a thing?"

"I guess, maybe. I don't know. I have a lot going on right now."

"So, let me guess, Darla; you want to drop it?"

I nod in agreement. "Definitely."

After lunch, I have P.E. and, as luck would have it, we are starting a unit on swimming. So, we all had to bring swimsuits to school.

The last thing I want to do is go into the water, but Mr. Sperry is the wrestling coach, and maybe if he sees how athletic I am, he will let me try out for the wrestling team. Well, at a minimum, it's a chance to impress him, and I'll take every chance I can get to do that.

We start class with Mr. Sperry asking, "Who here knows how to swim?"

Everyone raises their hand except for two boys who I don't know.

Mr. Sperry says, "Okay, well, let's do a swimming test in the shallow end of the pool. Just swim from one side to the other, staying in the shallow end, please."

As soon as I get in the water, I get flashbacks from yesterday. At least, I think that is what is happening. I get flooded with emotions again. I feel nervousness, anxiety, anger, boredom, and indifference. It's kind of distracting. I swim side-to-side, though, with ease.

Mr. Sperry says, "Pass. Go to line one."

There are basically two lines; one for those who can swim, and one for those who cannot. In the end, the class is split in half. Several of us are good swimmers, and then there are the not-so-good swimmers. So, the not-so-good swimmers are sent to the shallow end to work on back floating, and the stronger swimmers are sent to the deep end to work on diving.

We are just doing simple dives into the water, and then we get out of the water, back in line, and do it again. Because the pool is indoors at Grinwell, we don't really get cold getting out of the water like we would if we were outside. This is actually pretty relaxed and enjoyable. Unfortunately, Mr. Sperry has to spend most of his time in the shallow end, helping people learn the basics. That makes sense but doesn't give me much of a chance to stand out.

We end class by treading water. Mr. Sperry has decided to make that a competition to see who can tread water the longest in the deep end. One at a time, people give up and swim to the ladder to get out of the pool. Of course, there are always the wise guys who immediately go under and tap out. Mr. Sperry doesn't think too much of that. He says, "Is that the best you've got? That's ridiculous." So that adds some pressure. But, to be honest, treading water is easy for me.

Eventually, I am the last one left in the water, and Mr. Sperry blows the whistle and raises my arm up, announcing me as the winner, which is kind of a cool feeling because that is exactly what happens in wrestling when a winner is declared. He may do that out of habit—I don't know—but I like it.

"Good job, Ms. Towns. You look like you could have kept going all day." Then he turns to the class and says, "Treading water is an important skill to have if you are going to be out on the water. All of you need to take this as seriously as Ms. Towns next time."

As soon as class is over, I head over to Coach Sperry.

"Yes, Ms. Towns?"

"Thanks for what you said in class."

"I meant it. Treading water is important," Mr. Sperry says.

"No, I meant about me doing a good job."

"I meant that, too."

I just blurt it out, "I wanted to talk to you about trying out for the wrestling team."

"Well, it's a really good team, as you know. It's one of the highest rated in our class in the state. The competition for a spot on the team is going to be tough."

"I know, but I spent several years doing jiu jitsu with my dad, and I'm pretty good at it."

"Well, that's helpful, but jiu jitsu and wrestling, while similar, are still different enough to maybe not translate. I'm not sure it's a great idea for you to try out."

As he turns to walk away, I decide I am not going to let this opportunity slip by. I'm still soaking wet, but that is going to have to wait. I demand, "You *need* to let me try out for the team, Mr. Sperry."

He turns around slowly, scratching his head, and says, "You know what? You should try out for the team. Why not? We will post tryouts soon, just make sure you grab a permission slip and have your parents sign it."

"Is one parent enough?" I ask.

"Sure, just have one of them sign the form"

"Thank you, Mr. Sperry."

"Don't thank me yet. You are a long shot to make the team, at best, Ms. Towns."

"A long shot is better than no shot."

Mr. Sperry replies, "Indeed."

Team Managers

Jon

WHAT A GREAT DAY. OTHER than the brief incident with Brad, which turned out far better than expected, even if I did bend our Bragi rules a little bit. Since he really did see egg on my pants, I technically am not allowed to clean them in a way that cannot be explained. However, nobody is saying anything or questioning it. The only thing I heard through the grapevine is that Brad got put in his place by Sam. That is a good and a bad thing. It may make him even more inclined to really go after me. I guess time will tell. For now, it's a win, and I'll take it.

Speaking of wins, the biggest win of the day came from the time I spent with Darla. I am concerned, though, because something is definitely bothering her, and it must be serious if she doesn't want to talk about it. She also needed to be held, so whatever it is must have scared her, at least some. I'll have to tread lightly, because if she doesn't want to say something, I can't and don't want to make her. I'm sure she will tell me in her own way and on her terms. For now, I'll just make sure she knows that I am here for her and that I care.

I care. That's a new feeling for me. I have a girl who I care deeply for, who is not Jess. A smile comes to my face just thinking about her. Darla, thinking about Darla.

I am leaning against my locker, contemplating all of this, when I hear, "What's the stupid grin for, Bragg?" Of course, it is Brad and his posse.

"Nothing. I was just thinking about how nice it is to have clean pants." Probably not the smartest thing to say, but it is the first thing that pops into my head and, for some reason, my filter fails me.

Everyone around thinks I'm pretty funny, but not Brad.

"Very funny, Bragg. I don't know what you did or how you did it, but I *know* your pants were messed up. I'm keeping my eye on you. You better watch your back."

Sam comes along just in time to hear that and replies, "Don't worry, Jon; I have your back."

Marc is with him, as well, and says, "Yeah, me, too."

Brad gives Sam a dirty look then walks away, shaking his head.

"Hey, football tryouts are about to start. Why don't you and Marc come?" Sam says.

"Oh, we aren't into sports, Sam," Marc replies.

"You never know, you might like it."

"Oh, we know." I chuckle. "We get enough in gym class, but we will come with you. Maybe the coach can use a couple of team managers."

"Yeah, yesterday after school, nobody was there to help out the coaches. It was just everyone who wanted to be on the team. If you are interested, I'll vouch for you with the coaches, if it helps," Sam says.

"Thanks, Sam. It sounds like the coaches don't have a lot of options, so we should be good. Marc and I will be right there."

As soon as they leave, Marc asks, "What are you doing? I don't want any part of the football team."

I respond, "You mean, what are *we* doing? We are going to keep an eye on Sam and the rest of the team to see if we spot any giant behavior."

"Nice." Marc nods. "An undercover operation. I do like those. What about Jill?"

"Oh, Jill told me she was going to get some extra practice in with Jess before cheer tryouts."

The football coach doesn't actually teach at the school; all he does is coach football. His name is Coach Adams, and while he is young, he demands respect. The guys immediately give it to him, too, because he has a really sweet sports car that is easily the coolest car in the parking lot, and we can all hear it when he starts up the engine wherever we are in the school. It is quite loud, too loud if you ask me. Anyway, he's kind of a tough guy with what appears to be an intentional constant five o'clock shadow on his face.

We cautiously walk up to him before practice, and he says, "Get in your practice gear, boys."

"Sorry, Coach, we aren't here to try out for the team," I tell him.

"Okay, so why are you wasting my time then?"

Marc says, "We were wondering if you could use a couple of team managers to help with towels, water, or whatever you need."

"As a matter of fact, we could. Why don't you boys go over by the bench to talk to Coach Wilkerson and see how you can help him with tryouts today."

We both say, "Yes, sir, Coach sir!"

"Just coach is fine, boys."

The sun is high in the sky, and the heat is almost unbearable. The humidity makes it feel like you're swimming through the air. It's the kind of day where you can feel the sweat trickling down your back, even if you're just standing still.

Coach Wilkerson, a stocky man with a booming voice, immediately puts us to work. "All right, boys, I need you to fill up these water bottles and make sure they're always full every day. The team's going to need to stay hydrated."

We head to the field, lugging the heavy cooler and filling up about fifty water bottles. The players are already doing their warm-ups, running laps around the field. Sam stands out like a giant among men, his broad shoulders and towering height screaming intimidation.

The first drill is a tackling drill. Each player takes turns trying to get past Sam without getting tackled. He smashes them all but always helps each one up and pats them on the shoulder pads. It's impressive to watch, and even more so to see how he manages to be both a powerhouse and a good sport.

Next, they move on to sprints down the field. Starting at the goal line, they go to the ten and back, then the twenty, and so on, all the way to the end of the field. Sam, being a head above everyone else and about twice as wide, still beats everyone easily. His speed is astonishing for someone his size. It's like watching a freight train with the agility of a sprinter.

Finally, they do throwing drills. Sam steps in and throws as well as Brad, QB1. There are some whispers from the players as everyone is shocked to see Brad being challenged. After they are done, Coach Adams asks if Sam is interested in being a quarterback.

"No, but I am interested in being a tight end and going both ways as a linebacker."

Throughout the practice, Sam continues helping everyone up from the field when they are down and goes out of his way to make everyone feel a part of the team. If he is a giant, he is nothing like Dustin or Coach Locke, that's for sure. He genuinely seems to care about literally everybody.

As practice ends, the players are tired but energized. Sam is surrounded by his new teammates (aka new worshipers), and it's clear that he's already made a strong impression.

Coach Adams gathers everyone for a final pep talk, emphasizing the importance of teamwork and determination.

Marc and I retire to the bleachers, sitting down with a sigh of relief.

"Man, who knew being a team manager was such hard work?" Marc says, wiping sweat from his forehead.

"Tell me about it," I reply. "But we got what we came for. Sam is definitely different. Whether he's a giant or not, he's anything but average."

Marc nods. "Yeah, but he's a good guy. I didn't see anything that would make me think he's dangerous."

"Same here. That said, I have been wrong about that before, that's for sure."

The sun starts to set, casting long shadows across the field. The heat of the day begins to fade, replaced by a cool, refreshing breeze. I take a deep breath, feeling a sense of accomplishment. Tomorrow is another day, and who knows what it will bring? For now, I'm content with the knowledge that I have good friends and a purpose. Life is good.

As Marc and I walk back to my car, we talk about the day's events.

"You know, Jon, we might actually enjoy being team managers," Marc says with a grin.

I laugh. "Yeah, who would have thought? It's not so bad after all."

There is a note from Jill on the car.

I got a ride home from Jess. See you waterboys there.

Ah, a love letter from Jill. Just when you need someone to give you a nice stiff jab to the ego, she never disappoints.

Bloody Hair

Darla

AFTER A LONG DAY, I'M looking forward to getting home and spending time with Dad in the fields. Whenever I have a lot on my mind, spending time with him helps. He listens, and he is always there for me. Dad is fully present for any conversation and isn't too "judgy" about anything. He simply listens and offers the best advice he can think of, given whatever the circumstances happen to be. I'm thinking he is the best one to talk to about the lake. I know Mother said not to, but what Mother doesn't know isn't going to hurt her. Plus, she can't always get what she wants.

As the cousins and I pile into the Tahoe to head home, I take my place in the back. Clearly, Gaddy is going to be driving, so I'm just going to give that to her. It's not worth the fight or whatever she may end up doing to get me to agree to it. I don't want anyone else to possibly overhear her ordering me around and get any ideas. I don't want to be embarrassed, and I don't want anyone else to think I am okay with being treated that way.

Just as we settle in, we get a text from Mother to meet at Harmony Grove again. I am immediately filled with a burning desire to get out of this car.

I speak up and say, "I think I left a book in my locker. I'll be right back."

As I start to get out of the Tahoe, I hear another silent order booming from Gaddy, "*Sit back down! You are not going anywhere!*"

Once again, my body involuntarily obeys.

I hate this feeling—the feeling of being completely present and knowing exactly what is going on but not being able to do a thing about it. It's an incredibly helpless feeling, almost as bad as when I was captured at scout camp in the summer. I feel equally as violated.

I do not want this to be my life. In fact, it is not going to be my life. I decide to fight this right here and right now. Darla Towns is nobody's plaything and is not to be messed with like this.

I push past the control as we pull out of the school parking lot and shout, "Stop! Stop this right this instant!"

To my surprise, Gaddy slams on the brakes and stops so suddenly that the car behind us bumps into us. We all get out to survey the damage.

I contemplate making a break for it but know now that we are definitely going to have to explain this to Mother.

The girl who hit us from behind is crying hysterically. I don't know her, but she says her name is Tonya. That's all we can get out of her. There is really just a scratch on the Tahoe and the same on her car, which is an older VW bug. She just keeps saying that her parents are going to kill her.

Olga takes a few drinks of water then walks over to Tonya, telling her, "Everything is going to be fine. There is just a small scratch on your front bumper. Your parents probably won't even notice. In fact, you don't need to say anything to anyone."

Tonya immediately stops crying and regains her composure. "You're right. Thank you. I was just being silly. I can be quite dramatic."

Olga says, "Oh, it's all good. We know it can be scary when you get into a little fender bender. Don't feel bad. Everything is peachy."

"Thank you," Tonya says. "I'll see you around school." With that, she waves, gets into her car, and drives away, looking right as rain.

I turn to Olga with a bit of panic and confusion over what just happened. "Did you just control that girl somehow? Also, did I cause Gaddy to stop? Is this a two-way type of thing?"

Olga touches me on the arm, and I immediately feel calm. "We'll talk about this later."

"Yeah, maybe later is better."

With that, we get into the Tahoe again, and I'm starting to wonder if I am being controlled when I don't even know it. I mean, Tonya was just controlled and didn't know it. Maybe that has been happening to me. That would not be okay. That is not okay. I have to say something.

"You shouldn't do that to people."

"Do what?" Olga asks. "You mean, make them feel better when they are scared, panicking, and making a scene?"

"Control them," I correct her. "It's not fair. People should not be manipulated like that."

"She didn't seem to mind. In fact, she looked and felt great when she left. What's wrong with that?"

I'm getting nowhere, so I throw my hands up in surrender. "I give up with you guys."

As we come to a stop at Harmony Grove, I see Mother is already there. She has drawn a large circle with some symbols inside of it. There are eight drawings and one in the center. It looks a little like what you see in movies for witch rituals. I'm immediately not looking forward to whatever is about to happen.

As soon as we get out of the Tahoe, I feel the pull of the water, and a flood of emotions coming from it rush to me again. The strongest of these feelings is a tense anxiety. There is uncertainty in the air, but I do feel a rush of power come over me. I feel really strong suddenly.

Hef says to me, "It feels great, doesn't it?"

I shrug again. "It's all right, I guess."

Then I hear, in unison, all of the cousins in my head saying, *"Water is your friend. It's your everything."*

As we march toward Mother, I wonder what that means.

Mother, as if she hears my thoughts, says, "I'll tell you what we mean when we say water is your everything. As the daughter of the waves, your powers are strongest when you are surrounded by large masses of water, especially this lake. We'll talk about that more later, but for tonight, I need a volunteer to go to the middle of the circle, and I need the rest of you to join hands with me around the circle, one step inside each symbol."

Of course, Gaddy, ever the mother brown-noser, immediately volunteers.

Mother accepts her and motions her to the center of the circle. "Okay, we will start with you, Blodughadda."

I reluctantly join hands to complete the circle, with Olga holding one hand and Mother the other.

Mother says, "We gather together today, the women of the sea, and call upon our ancestors to hear our pleas for power. We are all here, and we are ready to work with you."

With that, a rush of power hits me as if I were shocked. Not a bad shock, just like it feels when you are walking around the house and touch a doorknob. It's a little pop, and then I feel incredible. The water has risen from its banks and is surrounding us all, about ankle-deep then knee-deep. I know the spark I felt hit me when the water touched me.

This incredible feeling is short-lived, though, because, in the water, I feel a massive amount of pain and suffering. It hits me hard. It's like a thousand knives are slicing into me but, at the same time, not hurting me. I just feel cut after cut and feel someone, or something, is in pain.

As we stand there, I can't believe my eyes. The water all around us is bloodred, and there are dead fish everywhere. Is that the pain

I feel? I know instantly it is. I feel the pain the fish are feeling. It is overwhelming. So much so that I release Olga's hand and break the tight grip Mother has on my hand.

Immediately after doing that, the pain stops, and as the water recedes, it carries the fish out into the lake. I see a distinct circle of blood make its way out to the middle of the lake.

Mother looks at me in anger, pointing out toward the lake. "Bara, *never* break the bond before we are finished. Look what you did now!"

"What *I* did?" I reply. "Did you see all of those fish? They were in immense pain."

"We'll talk about this later. For now, help me remove all traces of the circle. We need to get out of here. There's no way we can explain that."

We do as we are told.

When I get back into the Tahoe with the cousins, there is an energy in the air. We all feel it. I can tell without talking to them that they feel it, too. My biggest concern is I saw what we did, and I know it was wrong, but it also felt amazing. A wave of guilt hits me over feeling so good after doing something so terrible as killing so many fish.

As we get farther from the lake, the flood of feelings slows down to a trickle, and I feel relief. At the same time, I can feel a single tear sliding down my face.

What have we just done?

Cry Babies

Jon

SINCE WE'RE LATER THAN normal getting home, Mother meets us at the door and asks, "Where were you two?"

"Sorry, Mom, I should have texted. Marc and I decided to be team managers for the football team," I explain, trying to sound nonchalant.

"Oh, Jon, that's great. I'm glad to see the two of you showing your school spirit. Is that going to be a big-time commitment?"

"I guess. It's pretty much as much time as being on the team. We have to be at every practice, and we are there kind of late cleaning up after everyone."

"Have the boys been good to you? The boys on the team?" she asks with a hint of concern.

"I mean, it was just one practice so far, but they were cool. One of the new kids from Bluehill that we met at scout camp encouraged us to get involved. He's a good guy and probably the best player on the team."

"Oh really? Even better than Brad Dillon?"

"Yeah, even better than Brad."

"Interesting. Well, get washed up. Dinner is on the table."

We don't need to be told twice. It's been a long day, and we're starving.

We drop our bags and take turns washing our hands in the powder room. With that, we head straight to the table.

Yes! Mom's famous fried chicken. That's perfect. Marc and I both love drumsticks, so we each grab a leg and start eating while we're still passing the rest of the food. That's the best part of a chicken leg—the convenience of being able to hold it in one hand and grab more food with the other. It's so efficient and delicious.

After we have our fill of corn, mashed potatoes, and chicken, Marc and I down the last bit of milk in our glasses and start to clear the table. We were late enough that everyone else already ate. Accordingly, the rule in our house is the last to eat clears the table. So, we help Mom put the leftovers away in the fridge and load the dishwasher.

As we're finishing, Grandpa walks by the kitchen on his way downstairs and motions for Marc and me to join him. Of course, we're more than happy to do so. Mom excuses us, and we head downstairs with Grandpa to fill him in on our day.

Grandpa asks, "Do you still have the egg?"

Wow, I almost forgot about the egg. So much has happened that that seems like last week.

"Oh, actually, no. The strangest thing happened. I ducked into the bathroom because something felt different about the egg. How I knew that, I still don't know. In any event, I made sure nobody was around, and then said a rhyme, asking Odin to break the spell."

"What happened next?" Grandpa asks.

"Well, I got interrupted by one of the kids at school. He's not particularly nice to me, and he shoved me into the sink. The egg broke in my pants."

"It really did break? Brad wasn't lying?" Marc asks.

"Yeah, it broke."

I give Marc a look, as if to say *just let it go*. I don't really want to tell Grandpa that I used a rhyme to clean my pants because, technically, I'm not supposed to do that. I intend to let that detail just get lost in the moment.

Grandpa asks, "That's it? What happened before that?"

"Nothing." I shrug.

"That's strange. Are you sure nothing happened?"

"Yep, pretty sure."

"Huh. Well, Odin usually requires a strong show of emotion, like I said last night. A truly selfless act to grant someone the ability to break a protection spell. It's like a test, showing that you are a good person and have true intentions."

My mind retraces my steps, and all I can think of is Darla. I was there for her, and we had a moment. Was that something that would count as a selfless act of love?

Love? Am I ready to talk about this? I guess I kind of have to.

"Well, I did talk with Darla right before that. She was scared about something, and I just listened to her."

"Interesting. She must be a special girl to you," Grandpa says with a slight smile and a twinkle in his eye. Then he continues, "Well, I did hear back from the APS on skinwalkers and the DNA from scout camp. They did say it depends upon what type of skinwalker we are dealing with, but it is possible. Their advice is to just keep an eye on the subject and report back."

"Roger that. That's why we joined the football team as team managers. We want to keep our eye on Sam and also see if anyone else might fit the profile of a giant. I can say, if Sam is a giant, he certainly is the nicest one I have ever met. He genuinely seems to care about everyone. He's a really good person, from what I can tell."

Grandpa nods. "Well, that's good news. I guess just keep an eye on him."

"That's the plan," Marc says.

Marc and I don't have much time for Bragi training. Accordingly, we have to cut it short tonight so we can get our homework done, play a few games, and drop Marc off. We just need to keep doing what we're doing and see what turns up. We know there is a giant in the area; we just need to figure out if that giant is Sam.

I WAKE UP READY TO face the day. I am going to try to see if I can connect with Darla again this morning. I just want to check in on her.

As I walk through the hall by her locker, she's not there. I walk back and forth, trying to look busy, but really, I am just waiting for her. It doesn't look like today will be the day I find out what is bothering her. It's disappointing, but I tried.

The school day is the first in a long time where nothing embarrassing happens. Brad doesn't bother me, I don't trip and fall, and everyone treats us differently. Is this because we are part of the team now? Was it really that easy? That would have been good to know before I got Bragi powers. It could also be because of Sam being around us. I'm not sure, but I could get used to this.

After school, Marc and I head out to fill up water bottles for practice. On the way, we run into Jess, Gaddy, Ronny, and Jill at the water fountain.

"Hey, ladies, fancy meeting you here."

"We are heading to cheer tryouts, and I advised the girls to fill up their water bottles before going," Jess says. "We always run out of water at cheer sessions. We don't have hundreds of water bottles like the football team."

"Can we have one of yours?" Gaddy asks.

"Oh no, sorry, these are for the football team," Marc tells her.

Then Gaddy and Ronny clasp hands and start a cheer.

> "Don't be sad, don't shed a tear,
> Drama queens, the end is near!
> Grinwell-Bluehill, fierce and strong,
> We'll take the win; it won't take long!"

After they finish, they look at each other and giggle, and then they say in unison, "Go team!"

As they walk off, Jill sticks out her tongue as she goes by last.

Marc just shakes his head. "Lame. Girls are so weird."

The guys have been running for a bit because it took us a while to get all the bottles and the cooler filled. They run over and start drinking as soon as Coach lets them. They get their fill then turn to head back out. Sam notably stays on the field the whole time.

I guess he doesn't need water. That's strange, right?

Anyway, Coach decides to run a drill where everyone squares off one at a time and faces a defender to see if they can get past them. Of course, Sam is the defender. One at a time, they all try to evade him and get tackled. Then, oddly, each of them starts crying after they get tackled. It's quite the sight. Actually, it's hilarious to Marc and me, but the coaches ... not so much.

Coach Adams is beside himself. He just keeps yelling, "There is no crying in football!" I don't know if he realizes he is repeating a line from a Tom Hanks movie or not, but he's sticking with it. Followed by, "You drama queens are never going to make the team."

The problem is everyone is doing the same thing, and Coach has to let some of them be on the team.

As practice ends, Coach gives a lecture on football not being a sport for the weak. He wants all of them to go home and think about their actions, which of course leads them to start crying again.

Coach just turns his back, shaking his head, and walks off toward the locker room and to his office.

Marc and I look at each other, trying hard not to laugh because Coach Wilkerson is still there, and we can tell that now is not the time. I just lean toward Marc and say, "Now *that* was weird."

Marc shrugs. "Football players aren't as tough as I thought, that's for sure."

Compromise

Darla

TODAY IS THE DEADLINE for signing up for several extracurricular activities. This is new to many of the students because, when the schools were separate, there wasn't really any competition. At Bluehill, if you wanted to try anything, you absolutely could. There was almost no barrier to entry, and the coaches or teachers involved were just happy to have anyone participate. That's not the case this year. The competition is going to be real, and everyone is talking about it. That does not deter recruiting, though; it's in full force.

Jess was devastated this morning when I told her that I wasn't going to try out for the cheer team. I know that is something she has been planning all summer, but it just isn't where my heart is this year. I have other plans, and if I am going to make the wrestling team, I need to hit the weight room and start a serious conditioning regimen. The Grinwell wrestling team has always been the best in the district, so Coach is right—there will be stiff competition at every weight class.

Jess was half-relieved and half-concerned when Gaddy and Ronny told her that they would be trying out for the cheerleading team. I should say Gaddy told Jess because it was pretty clear that she voluntold Ronny that she was doing it.

Ronny follows Gaddy around like a lost puppy, so there's no way she'll challenge that decision. She'll fall right in line like the good little soldier she is. Besides, Gaddy would most likely just command her to do it, anyway.

We all decide that it makes sense for all of us to choose some after-school activity because we are carpooling, and it's unlikely that Mother would want us to take multiple trips every night to and from the farm. So, with that, Olga, Duff, and Hef are joining the swim team; Billow and Nora are going to play volleyball; and Liv is going to sing in the choir. I am just going to work on getting into wrestling shape and see if there is any way to work out with the wrestlers after school while we wait for the season to get started.

Tonight is the first night of all of this, and I am making good use of the time. I am working on strength training, which normally would be easy, but with so many sports, the weight room is flooded. It takes quite a bit of time to get on any machine, and when people have one, they tend to sit on them—literally. It would be really nice if some teacher or coach would volunteer to direct the flow of traffic in the weight room. If this doesn't change, I may have to find another way to kill time after school.

Not surprisingly, we are summoned to the lake again after we are done for the day. We all pile into the Tahoe and head to Harmony Grove to meet Mother. You would think that a bunch of girls in a car would be fine and that it would smell good or at least okay. Let me tell you that that is not the case with this bunch. It's the smell of chlorine and sweat all rolled together with the only one not emitting an offensive odor being Liv, our in-car DJ and resident musician. So, tonight, I am more than happy to exit the Tahoe when we arrive at the lake.

I stroll over to where Mother is standing as a fresh idea pops into my head. "Mother, I would like to propose a compromise on our little stalemate here."

"What makes you think you have a choice?" she says.

"Well, maybe I don't have a choice, but what I am talking about is me being a willing participant."

That gets her attention. "Go on then."

"I propose that you let me try out for the wrestling team and, in return, I agree to participate in these water exercises or whatever you call them."

Whether she intends to actually go through with it or not, she doesn't hesitate for a second as she says, "I'll take that deal, Darla. However, if you don't willingly participate every single day, then the deal is off, and I'll make sure you are right back on the dance team. That's where you belong, anyway."

Whatever. She doesn't know me well if she thinks that is where I belong.

"Darla, you need to get used to the fact that we can hear each other's thoughts when we are around the water. I think I know my daughter. She may get confused from time to time, but she will obey."

Darn it, stupid hive mentality got me again. Ugh, and again, Mother just looks at me, acknowledging my series of mistakes.

"Now that Darla has agreed to join us, we are going to talk about tonight's training. Tonight, you girls are to gather around me."

We all gather around Mother, holding hands as she closes her eyes and speaks. "I am the goddess of the sea, and these are my daughters. As you wished, we have come together to pay homage and show our respect to you. We call the gods and giants to us. It is nearing time for us to be restored. Help my daughters understand and grow into their powers, for they will all be needed."

As Mother speaks, the water once again rises from its banks to greet us. As soon as it touches me, I can feel excitement, and I can tell it is coming from the cousins and Mother. I also feel something else, something dull, something more of an ache. I got it. I feel doubt. One of the cousins has doubts.

Mother speaks up, "For any of my daughters who has doubts, help them to see the virtue in what we are doing and how important each of them is to our mission. There is no room for doubt as we have waited for centuries for this time to come. We are here, and together, we will be restored." With that, Mother opens her eyes. She then says, "You must not tell anyone what we are doing. They will know soon enough. For now, this is not to leave this group."

"What about Dad? I can talk to him, right?"

"*No! No, you may not.*" Mother is staring straight at me, and I can hear her thoughts loud and clear. "*Do not question me, Darla. This is not open for discussion or compromise or any wiggle room at all.*"

I was going to say it, but what is the point? I'll just think it. "*I get it, Mother. I won't tell Dad.*"

I honestly don't know what Mother is going on about. What are we supposedly being restored to? What is her endgame here? Why do we have to be at the lake? Why *this* lake? I have so many questions and so few answers.

Mother looks at me and says, "Thanks for asking, Darla."

We all continue to stand in a circle, and Mother begins to tell us, "Ran is known for her net, which she uses to capture sailors who venture too far into her domain. She is both a protector and a treacherous force, embodying the dual nature of the sea."

I feel a shiver run down my spine as she speaks. The legend of Ran is both fascinating and terrifying. The idea of a net dragging sailors to the depths below, where they are lost forever, is haunting. It's a reminder of the power and unpredictability of the sea, something I am starting to understand more with each visit to the lake.

As Mother finishes her story, she looks at each of us. "Remember, we are bound by the sea. Our strength comes from the water, and we must honor it. Tonight's training is just the beginning. You will each learn to harness your powers and understand the depths of your abilities. Together, we will achieve greatness." With that, she dismisses us.

I feel a mixture of relief and apprehension as the water recedes, leaving us standing on the shore.

As we head back to the Tahoe, I can't shake the feeling that there is so much more to learn, so much more to understand. The legend of Ran and her daughters lingers in my mind, a constant reminder of the need to know more.

Liv starts playing music as we drive away, and I let the rhythm of the songs wash over me. The night air is cool and refreshing, a stark contrast to the heated intensity of our training. I glance out the window at the darkened landscape, wondering what the future holds for us. Mother's words echo in my mind, and I know that this is just the beginning of a journey that will change everything. Plus, she is going to let me wrestle. That's a good—no, great—deal.

Boy Cries Wolf

Jon

AS WE DESCRIBE WHAT happened in practice to Grandpa, he just nods. Then he asks, "So, nobody touched the water between when you filled it up and when the players drank it, right?"

"No, sir, I don't think anybody touched the water. Just Marc and me. Why?"

"Well, if Sam was the only one who didn't drink the water and he was the only one not acting emotional, it sounds like something may have been in the water. Can you bring some water home tomorrow from the fountain?"

"We were thinking that we should try to get Sam to drink some, and then maybe you could send it to the APS for testing?" Marc explains. "Would that be enough for testing?"

"You and Jon do that. I think we need to know exactly what is in that water. Speaking of which, there was a problem at the lake that the APS was called about. Jon, we need to go to meet them. There was a large red spot in the middle of the lake, and it turns out a bunch of fish died. We don't know why, and we need to use your gift to see what happened."

We all drive to meet the APS at Harmony Grove. They are concerned enough that they sent a field unit from Chicago to check it out. When we get there, there are dozens of fish—or, I guess, fish parts—captured in a net that has been pulled out of the lake.

An APS agent comes over and says, "We collected the best specimens we could and laid them over here. We need to know what they saw before they died."

I walk over to the fish and stare into their eyes. I remember reading that many fish have dark eyes because of the melanin in their retinas. Some fish can have eyes that look golden, silver, or even red, which helps them see better in different lighting. This variation in eye color helps them adapt to their environments. These fish are no different, and their eyes appear black, a typical adaptation for Iowa lake fish.

> "As I look into your pitch-black eyes,
> I need to know what happened to you.
> I'm sure it really was quite the surprise,
> And that you would like to know, too."

With that, I see a flashback from each of the fish. I am able to see their final moments, just like I have with so many other animals. However, fish don't see a lot, and they don't see far. They typically only see a few feet in front of them. It's common for them to use their other senses to navigate the waters and pursue food.

I turn to Grandpa and the agent. "Not much. They just don't see very far, and their angle isn't a good one. I see several feet and legs, but nothing distinct, and it is brief. It could be boys on the beach; it could be a bunch of girls. I just can't tell. However, I don't see any explosions or weapons of any kind. It's like they were swimming toward something, and then they just died."

"That's strange," the agent says. "We are going to take these back to the lab in Chicago for some additional testing. I'll let you know if we find anything."

We each shake the agent's hand then head back to the Corolla. However, as we are about to get into the car, I see something in the woods. I motion to Grandpa and Marc to see if they see it, too.

"Do you see a large animal over there?"

They both nod, and Grandpa whispers, "Yes, let's see if we can get closer."

As we approach the beast, we notice that it is not afraid at all. Like many of the animals around here, it seems used to humans.

The woods around Harmony Grove are dense and dark, even in daylight. Tall trees with thick canopies block much of the sunlight, creating an eerie, shadowy atmosphere. The underbrush is covered with ferns and bushes, making it hard to see far. The air is thick with the scent of pine and damp earth, and the occasional rustle of leaves or snap of a twig adds to the feeling of being watched.

As we draw nearer, I start to ready myself for a fight. I get right up next to it, and find it is a wolf. A giant wolf. He is looking straight at me and isn't batting an eye.

"Hey there, big guy. Where are you from?" I reach up to try to touch him when I hear from behind me, "Whoa. What's that?"

I glance back, and it's the APS agent we were talking to.

When I turn back around toward the wolf, he's gone. It's like he disappeared.

"Well, I thought it was a wolf, but I didn't see it leave, and I didn't hear it run." Turning to Grandpa and Marc, I ask, "You saw it, too, right?"

Marc says, "Yeah, it was a massive wolf, and it wasn't afraid of us at all."

The agent turns to Grandpa and asks, "You think that was your skinwalker? Have you ever heard of a skinwalker doing something like what happened to the fish?"

"No—I mean, yes," Grandpa says. "Yes, I think that could have been a skinwalker, and no, I've never seen or heard of one of their kind spontaneously killing fish. Why would they? They clearly don't need to. That wolf was enormous."

"We are going to comb the woods to see if we can collect any wolf scat or other DNA. I'd like to track that thing down," the agent says.

"Be careful," Grandpa warns. "They tend to travel in packs."

The agent nods, and then we head back to the car to go home.

We drive back mostly in silence, just taking in what we saw.

As we pull into Marc's driveway to drop him off, Grandpa says, "Don't forget to bring me some water from practice. We need to check this Sam out."

Marc nods. "We understand, and we will, Grandpa. Have a good night."

"Goodnight, Marc. See you tomorrow."

As we pull away, Grandpa says, "We are going to need to spend a few moments with the *Book of Bragi* when we get home. I have something to show you."

When we get back to the basement, Grandpa shows me some passages that relate to skinwalkers. As discussed, there are two varieties: the good, kind, and respectful skinwalkers from Odin, and then there are the others from Loki. As I read how to handle them both, I see that they are really different.

Grandpa says, "If you encounter a skinwalker, you may only have a split-second to decide their lineage. If you are wrong, it could end badly. If you are right, you can control them. The problem is the way to control each type is different. Controlling one from Odin takes a great show of empathy and kindness. To control one from Loki, you have to be the aggressor and put him on his back. You have to physically earn respect. You saw tonight how big they are and how dangerous that could be. Be careful, Jon. They have a lot of power."

I just nod, deep in thought. I didn't get any bad feelings from that wolf. In fact, I felt like we were best friends. Could that be a trick? I don't know, but somehow, I feel I am going to find out.

That night, I have a dream. It feels so real, more like a vision than a dream. I am standing in the woods near Harmony Grove. The trees are tall and dark, casting long shadows across the forest floor. The air is cool and damp, and I can hear the faint sound of water lapping against the shore of the lake in the distance.

Suddenly, the giant wolf appears in front of me. He stands still, staring at me with his intense, dark eyes. I feel a wave of calm wash over me, and then I hear a voice in my head. It's not a human voice, but I understand it perfectly.

"Jon, you are in danger. There is something coming, something dark and powerful. You must be prepared. Your friends, your family—they are all at risk."

"What is it? What's coming?" I ask, but the wolf doesn't answer. Instead, he looks at me with a mixture of sadness and urgency.

"You must trust your instincts. Trust the power within you. There is more to you than you realize. Remember, not all who appear friendly are truly so."

With that, the vision fades, and I wake up in my bed, drenched in sweat. My heart is pounding and, for a moment, I am convinced someone is in the room with me.

I sit up and look around, but there is no one there. The room is dark and still. However, I notice the window is open, and a cool breeze is blowing in. I get up and walk over to it, peering out into the night. The moon is full, casting an eerie glow over the landscape. I shut the window and latch it, just in case.

As I crawl back into bed, I can't shake the feeling that the wolf's warning was real. I lie there, staring at the ceiling, my mind racing with thoughts of what could be coming. Eventually, exhaustion takes over, and I drift back to sleep, but the wolf's words echo in my mind.

The Fog

Darla

THE MORNING SUN BEGINS to peek over the horizon, casting a soft golden light across the farm. The air is crisp, with just a hint of chill, signaling that a change in weather is coming. I take a deep breath, savoring the peacefulness of the early morning. The farm is still quiet, except for the gentle clucking of the chickens in the coop.

I pull on my work gloves and head to the chicken coop, carrying a bucket and a shovel. Cleaning out the chicken coop is a task I have done countless times, but it never feels routine. There's something soothing about the rhythmic nature of the work.

First, I unlatch the door to the coop and step inside, greeted by a flurry of feathers and curious clucks from the hens. Then I remove the old bedding, using the shovel to scoop out the soiled straw and wood shavings, dumping them into the bucket. It's important to get all the old bedding out to prevent the buildup of ammonia and bacteria, which can harm the chickens. The process is dusty and a bit smelly, but I don't mind. I know it's essential for keeping the chickens healthy and happy.

Once the old bedding is out, I take a broom and sweep the floor and nesting boxes, making sure every corner is clean. Next, I sprinkle a thin layer of diatomaceous earth on the floor of the coop. It's a natural powder that helps control mites and other pests. I spread it evenly, making sure to cover the entire floor and the nesting boxes. After that, I add fresh bedding—soft, clean straw mixed with wood shavings. The fresh bedding smells sweet and clean, a stark contrast to the soiled bedding I just removed. I fluff it up, making sure it's comfortable for the chickens.

The whole process takes about an hour, but I don't rush. I enjoy taking my time, making sure everything is just right. I know from Dad that "happy, healthy chickens lay better eggs," and I take pride in my work.

As I finish up, I hear footsteps behind me and turn to see Dad walking over.

"Mornin', darlin'. It's a beautiful day, isn't it?"

"Good morning, Dad. It sure is."

He looks around the coop, nodding appreciatively. "You always do such a good job with the chickens. They're lucky to have you."

"Thanks, Dad. It's kind of therapeutic, you know?"

He chuckles. "I know what you mean. Listen, your mom told me the news. She said you're allowed to try out for the wrestling team. That's great news, darlin', but how did you manage to convince her?"

I feel a pang of guilt but push it aside. "I agreed to participate in something with the cousins and Mother."

"What's that, darlin'?"

I hesitate, remembering Mother's stern warning not to tell Dad. "Just some stuff by the lake."

Dad raises an eyebrow but doesn't press further. "I see. Well, I'm not sure what that means but just be careful."

Thinking he's talking about wrestling, I grin. "Those boys better be careful. I'm going to take them down—literally."

Dad laughs, a sound that always makes me feel warm inside. "That's my girl. I'm sure you will, darlin', but I meant with your mother."

"I will, Dad. Thanks."

Wait—does Dad know more?

Mother's words echo loudly in my head. "*Do not question me, Darla. This is not open for discussion.*"

I head back into the house with this morning's haul of eggs and get ready for school.

AS I GET TO MY LOCKER, I see Jon awkwardly walking up and down the hall. I'm sure that means he is waiting for me because as soon as he sees me, he waves excitedly then quickly puts his hand down.

"Hey, Jon, good morning. Did you need something?" I kind of like making Jon feel awkward. It's a little mean, but it's funny to see how quickly his face will turn red.

"Um, I was just ... I was just waiting to see you." He gives up trying to act too cool.

I let him off the hook. "It's good to see you, too, Jon."

I can see him relax a little. Then he leans in to whisper, "Do you have a second so we can talk in private?"

It seems important. "Sure, Jon, what's up?"

We head around the corner and duck into the art room. Nobody is there.

Jon begins, "I had this weird dream last night about a giant wolf. He warned me about a darkness that is coming and told me to follow my instincts. What do you think that means?"

I can tell he is serious, so I try to comfort him. "Sounds like just a dream, Jon. Do you normally get dreams like this? Do you think it's a Bragi thing?"

"I don't know, Darla. I don't know."

My mind immediately jumps to Dad's warning this morning, but instead of saying anything, I give him a quick hug and just say, "I'm sure it will be okay, Jon."

"Yeah, you're probably right. Thanks. I better run; I need to catch up with Sam."

"Oh, okay. See you later. Maybe keep the dream talk on the DL."

He nods as he heads out of the art room first. I follow a bit later. We don't want to give anyone the wrong idea. Well, I don't want to give them the wrong idea, or do I? You know what? I don't really care what people think. I like Jon.

Did I really just think that? What has gotten into me?

Throughout the day, I find myself scribbling in class whenever I get bored. I write my name, then Jon's name, then my first name and his last name. I write his first name and my last name. I then use a hyphenated name and decide I like that best.

Jenny leans over and says, "So, Darla Towns-Bragg is the winner?"

"Shut up! I was just—"

"Yeah, I know, Darla. I like Jon, too. I mean, I like Jon for you."

I've never been this type of girl. I have always been a bit of a tomboy, and the last thing on my mind has been boys, and certainly never any specific boy.

Maybe it is what we went through, but I trust Jon. I wish I could tell him more about what is going on with Mother and the cousins, but I'm not disobeying Mother. It's not worth losing out on wrestling.

Tonight, after school, I choose to run around the track and make this a cardio day. I'm going to need a lot of endurance for wrestling. I have never trained this hard for anything, but I always do what it takes. I'm a Towns, and we never back down from a challenge. I'm going to make the wrestling team if it's the last thing I do. It's got to happen. I have to push myself.

Afterward, we drive out to Harmony Grove for another show-and-tell session with Mother. As we all feel each of these, we start to all want to volunteer. Well, all except for me.

Next up is Billow, and Mother says, "Okay, Bylgja, you are up."

We all gather in the circle around Billow and call upon the water. It's really getting easier and easier. The water comes up to meet us and surrounds us. Billow is in the middle, and a mist or fog starts to appear. Before we know it, we can all feel the wetness of the fog as it surrounds us. The water seems oddly happy to be near us, and I start to understand it. It likes this feeling a lot.

The water feels powerful in this fog/mist form and is quickly growing. As Mother instructs us to release it, it goes back out over the lake, and we see how beautiful it is. No wonder it likes this feeling so much.

Wait—did I really just say that water likes this feeling? How silly is that? It may be ridiculous, but somehow, I just know it. The water is now actively participating in what we are doing.

Upon seeing how thick the fog is, Mother seems concerned. She calls upon Olga to get into the center. Then we all circle around Olga as the water once again rises to meet us. The fog is still thick, but as we stand there, holding each other's hands, a cool breeze begins to blow as I feel the water is peaceful and relaxed.

The fog starts to disperse. It isn't gone, but the breeze is just enough to clear the area, and as the water recedes, the fog completely vanishes, and the lake is clear again.

As we finish up, Mother says, "It is time. We are going to throw a party here at the lake on Saturday. I want all of you to invite as many kids from school as you can. Can you do that? We need this whole beach full, so do your best to get everyone to come."

What a strange request. We have literally never thrown a party—ever.

That keeps rolling around in my head as we drive home and pull into the driveway. Mother is right behind us in her car as we arrive.

We find that Dad is finished in the fields earlier than normal, and he walks out to greet us with his brows furrowed. He has a clear expression of concern as he looks at Mother, but she dismisses it and tells him not to worry. All is under control.

Lake Party

Jon

MARC AND GRANDPA LISTEN as I start our session tonight, telling them about my dream. Marc already knows, of course—I told him as soon as we got to school today and Jill ran off. So, he is chiming in as usual.

Marc says, "So, we are thinking that the wolf might be Sam and that maybe he is warning us that a Loki is coming."

Grandpa thinks for a minute. "I don't know about that. It could just be related to the wolf we saw last night. It's possible that it was just a dream. Was it that same wolf in your dream?"

"Yes, it was. Do you think that means anything?"

"I think that means we all saw a giant wolf, and something like that sticks with you," Grandpa says. "I'm surprised we all didn't dream about the wolf last night. Did you get the water bottle?"

"Yeah. I mean, barely. It's kind of hard to sneak a water bottle out of the locker room, especially since we were targeting one Sam drank out of. The water goes so quickly, and they pass them around one at a time. I'm not even really sure if Sam drank out of it directly or if he just squirted it in like everyone else."

"Well, I was more interested in the water, anyway. I'll send it off to the APS for testing."

Tonight, we spend more time studying skinwalkers and how to communicate with them when they are in animal form. Apparently, they are still able to think as a human, so the form they have taken on

146

is really irrelevant. They are still able to reason and behave normally, just in the body of an animal. That makes them easy to communicate with and even easier to control.

When it comes to practicing the rhymes, that's a bit harder. It's not like we have a spare skinwalker ready for me to test rhymes on, so I do my best with controlling small animals. It's not exactly the same, but no two animals are the same, either, and practice makes perfect.

Grandpa sets up a small maze on the floor, placing a tiny mouse at one end. "Jon, use your power of Bragi to guide this mouse through the maze."

I take a deep breath and focus on the mouse. I've done this before, but it's still a challenge every time. "Okay, here goes.

"With the wit of Bragi and guidance clear,
Turn to the left, little mouse, never fear.
Find your path through this winding maze,
Step by step, in a rhythmic phase."

The mouse hesitates then scurries forward, turning left as I directed. It's working!

I follow it closely with my eyes, ready to issue the next command.
"Now to the right, and then go straight,
Follow my voice; don't hesitate.
Through the turns and twists so tight,
Keep moving forward, guided by light."

The mouse navigates through the maze, making its way past the obstacles. It reaches a dead end, and I quickly adjust my rhyme.
"Turn around and go back quick,
Find the path that's less thick.
Right at the corner, then straight ahead,
Follow my voice where you're being led."

The mouse reverses course and finds the correct path, moving more confidently now. I feel a surge of satisfaction as it nears the end of the maze.

"Almost there, just a bit more.

You're doing great, explore and soar.

Straight ahead to the finish line.

You've done well, little one, you're fine."

The mouse reaches the end of the maze, and I let out a breath I didn't realize I was holding.

Grandpa smiles and nods approvingly. "Well done, Jon. You're getting better at this."

We hear a ding and realize it's just a phone. Marc gets a text from Taylor, inviting him to a party at the lake. Less than sixty seconds later, I get a text from Darla.

"*Jon, Mother says we are throwing a party at the lake Saturday. Will you go with me?*"

I don't waste any time responding. I type back, "*Of course. Sounds fun!*"

Marc looks up from his phone and grins. "Hey, we've been invited to the first big party of the year. This is huge."

I nod, feeling a mix of excitement and curiosity. "Yeah, it is. I wonder what they'll have us do. Should we bring anything? Will there be beach volleyball and other games, or what?"

Our phones continue to have messages flooding in. It's kind of strange. I guess what is strange is we are involved. Usually, when stuff like this happens at school, we only find out about it at school and usually only after it happened.

Grandpa excuses himself from the conversation, clearly not interested in teenage party logistics or listening to our phones dinging. Marc and I talk about everyone who might be coming and discuss how this might be an opportunity to try to find that wolf, as well.

I get a snap from Jenny. I honestly forgot we are connected on Snapchat. She asks, "*Are you going to the lake party? I know Darla would appreciate it.*"

I reply, "*Yeah, definitely. She asked me, as well.*"

She just responds with a smiley face.

I show it to Marc.

Marc smiles. "Bro, you two have been dancing around each other for months. Maybe this is your chance. You know, homecoming is coming up. You should ask her."

I blink in surprise. "Homecoming? I don't know, Marc. What if she says no?"

Marc shakes his head. "Come on, Jon. Do you really think she is going to say no?"

I shrug. "Beats me. But let's get through this party first."

As the evening winds down, I can't help but feel a bit anxious about the dream and the upcoming party. Should I ask Darla to homecoming? Does that have to be something extravagant—the whole asking her to homecoming thing?

That night, as I drift off to sleep, I find myself once again in the presence of the giant wolf. The dream feels vivid, almost too real.

The wolf stands before me, its eyes glowing with a noticeable light. I can hear its thoughts, not in words but in a deep, resonant voice that echoes in my mind.

"*I told you that darkness is coming from where you will least expect it. This darkness lives below the surface, and it is growing in power and controlled by someone with evil intentions.*"

I try to respond, but no words come out. Instead, I feel myself being pulled into the wolf's vision.

We are in the woods, the same woods near Harmony Grove. The wolf leads me deeper into the forest, where the trees grow thicker and the light dims. I can feel the presence of something malevolent lurking just out of sight.

The wolf stops at the edge of a dark clearing facing a beach. "*This is where it begins. Beware of the shadows, Jon. Trust your instincts.*"

I wake up with a start, my heart pounding. The room is dark and, for a moment, I'm disoriented. I glance around, half-expecting to see the wolf standing in the corner. But there's nothing there.

I get out of bed and walk over to the open window, again shutting it just in case. The cool night air gives me a slight shiver as I return to bed.

As I lie back down, I can't shake the feeling that the wolf's warning is significant. The dream felt too real to be dismissed as just my imagination. I try to push the thoughts away and get some rest, but sleep doesn't come easily. The wolf's message keeps replaying.

The next morning, I wake up feeling groggy and unrested. The dreams have left me with more questions than answers, and I can't shake the feeling that something big is about to happen.

As I get ready for the day, I make a mental note to talk to Grandpa and Marc about the dream. Maybe they can help me make sense of it.

Heading downstairs, I see Grandpa already at the breakfast table. He gives me a knowing look. "Rough night?"

"Yeah, you could say that. The wolf visited me again."

Grandpa's eyes widen. "*Again*? What did he say this time?"

"He warned me about a darkness that's coming from where we least expect it. He said below the surface. It's growing in power and controlled by someone with bad intentions."

Grandpa nods thoughtfully. "Below the surface. What surface? The ground? Is this a reference to a Norse myth? Is he referring to a realm below? And if so, which realm? Is it Hades?"

I shrug, feeling the weight of Grandpa's words. "I don't know. We need to be prepared."

As we finish breakfast and head out for the day, I can't help but feel a sense of urgency. The wolf's warning hangs over me like a dark cloud. I know we need to stay vigilant. Something is coming, and we need to be ready for it. Now I'm suspicious even of my own shadow.

Family Meeting

Darla

IN THE TAHOE ON THE way to school, Gaddy goes into full lecture mode about getting everyone to attend the lake party. "Mother wants us to make sure this party is a success, so we have to divide and conquer. Each of us needs to target different grades and get as many people to agree to come as possible."

I roll my eyes. She's acting like we're planning a military operation. Seriously, it's not that hard. Everyone loves a lake party.

Duff pipes in with, "I have an idea. I know exactly what to do to get everyone to come."

Gaddy, the eternal control freak, demands, "What's your plan?"

Duff giggles, or maybe it's more of a cackle. Either way, it sends shivers down my spine.

"You'll see."

Great. This is going to be an education.

When I get to school, Jon is waiting for me by my locker.

"So, a lake party, huh? Is that something of a Bluehill tradition? What inspired you?"

"Oh, it was most definitely *not* my idea," I object. "This is all Mother."

"But why is your mom interested in throwing a party for apparently most of the school?"

"Great question. I wish I had the answer. I guess it's just to make the cousins feel welcome."

151

"They seem to be getting along just fine, from what I can tell."

"Well, try convincing Mother of that." I really feel like I should tell him more about what's been going on, but it's not something I'm allowed to talk about. It's just too big of a risk with the whole hive mentality—I have no idea who might be listening. It feels really selfish, but I just can't take the chance. "At least it's a chance for us to spend some time together. That's a good thing, right, Jon?"

"Yes, that is definitely a good thing. I'm looking forward to it, Darla."

I decide to try to find the cousins to see what they're up to. When I get to ground level, I see Duff sucking down as much water as she can from the water fountain outside the main office. She guzzles it like she's been in a desert for days. Then, without hesitation, she opens the office door and hurries inside. She's only in there a minute or so before I overhear Mr. Douglas order everyone, "Out, and I mean *now*!" That seems like an odd thing for him to do before the school day starts, but I guess I don't know him.

Then I hear him clear his throat over the intercom and say, "Attention, please. I was just made aware of something incredibly disturbing, and it revolves around a lake party that I understand is happening at the end of the week at Harmony Grove. I want to express that this is not a school-sponsored event, and we forbid you from going." Then he abruptly ends with, "That's all."

This is not good. Mother is not going to be happy if we don't fill the beach up with kids. I'm not sure if I should call her or what the best course of action is right now. What would Mother do?

I can't even believe I just had that thought.

With that, I see Duff exiting the office, holding her throat and moving her hand around a bit to loosen it up. Whatever she did in there, she seems pretty happy with the result. Then she sees me and, as she walks by, says, "That should do the trick. There's nothing kids want to do more than go to a party that they are forbidden to go to."

"You intentionally told Mr. Douglas about Mother's party? Are you crazy?"

"No, I didn't say a word to him."

"Well, whatever you did, I think this might backfire. Good luck talking to Mother about this."

I am stressed out all day, thinking about what Mother is going to say when we get to the lake tonight. What could possibly be next for us? However, as we're pulling out of the school parking lot, we get a text from her that says, "*Change of plans. Meet at the house. ASAP!*"

Throughout the day, kids kept coming up to me, saying they're definitely going to be at the party because the principal is not going to tell them what to do. Scratch that—nobody is going to tell them what they can and can't do. It seems like Duff's plan actually worked, which just adds to my anxiety.

I'm still not entirely sure what happened, but I do know that I received a bunch of texts saying, "*I'm definitely coming now, etc.*" It seems Principal Douglas was our best party advertisement because nobody wanted to listen to him or be told what to do outside of school hours.

I can tell the cousins are happy with what we achieved but also upset because they wanted to do more training tonight, and they even try to make a pitch for us to go to Harmony Grove, anyway. There is no way that any of us want to deal with disappointing or upsetting Mother, however, so we head home.

Even more surprising is that Dad is also inside because the F-250 is parked in front of the house.

As we walk in, we find them sitting around the table with Dad at the head and Mother at the other end. Dad, surprisingly in control, asks everyone to please have a seat. He is always so kind and gentle; of course, we will sit for him.

As I grab the seat closest to him, he says, "Darlin' and girls, we need to talk about what all of you have been doing at the lake lately. Word is getting around that there are some unusual things happening, and that is bad for all of us."

Mother tries to jump in, but Dad holds his hand up to keep her silent. And. She. Stops.

Wow, good for you, Dad.

Then he starts in, "I want all of you to go around the table and tell me what your power is right now and who you inherited it from. I say this as a descendant of the giant Aegir, and your patriarch; therefore, you must tell me. *Do not be afraid*."

As his voice booms in our heads, we go around the table.

Gaddy speaks first. "I'm Gaddy, from Puntarenas, Costa Rica. I can kill animals in the water, just like my father."

Dad says, "Welcome, Blodughadda."

Gaddy proudly explains that she had always had a knack for scaring everything away. The fish the other night are just a taste of what she can do.

Billow is next. "I'm Billow, from Sydney, Australia. I can create mist or fog in the water, just like my mother."

Dad nods. "Welcome, Bylgja."

She has always loved the ocean and surfing, and she's always good at disappearing in the mist during early morning surfs.

Duff says, "I'm Duff, from Barcelona, Spain. I can bend my voice to sound like any other in the water, just like my mother."

Dad acknowledges her, "Welcome, Dufa."

Duff is always mimicking people and pranking them. Now it all makes sense, including what "Principal Douglas" said today.

Hef says, "I'm Hef, from Vancouver, Canada. I can make water swell and grow in volume, just like my mother."

Dad smiles. "Welcome, Hefring."

Hef is always causing waves when she's around water. She's the life of the party—literally.

Liv says, "I'm Liv, from Helsinki, Finland. I can become transparent with water, just like my father."

Dad nods. "Welcome, Himinglaeva."

Liv blends in every day at school and, honestly, I never see her around.

Ronny says, "I'm Ronny, from Galway, Ireland. I can control emotions through water, just like my mother."

Dad says, "Welcome, Hronn."

Ronny always seems to know exactly how to calm us down or rile us up, depending on her mood.

Olga speaks last, before me. "I'm Olga, from Bergen, Norway. I can manipulate the wind in water and calm animals down, just like my mother."

Dad nods. "Welcome, Kolga."

Olga has always loved the sea breeze and can whip up a storm just by walking along the shore.

Finally, he turns to me. "Darlin', what about you?"

I hesitate. "I'm Darla, from here. I think I can feel what things in the water are feeling, just like my father or my mother? I guess I have no idea how I got this power or which of you it came from."

Dad says, "Both, darlin'. Welcome, Bara."

Now that that is resolved, Dad continues, "We need to talk about some ground rules. While you are here, you will obey my orders, and note that includes Ran." He tips his head toward Mother. "We have been here for several years, and I do not want to jeopardize us getting outed for what we are. That could lead to the Asgardian Protection Society getting involved, and then we would be severely restricted. It's much better to self-regulate than to let the APS decide our fate. Is that understood?"

We all say, "Yes, sir," and he dismisses us.

As everyone gets up, he says, "Darlin', let's go for a walk. We have much to discuss."

Yeah, I think we do. I'm not sure out of everything that just happened what surprises me most—the fact that Dad is a giant or that he knows all about what the cousins and I can do. Him knowing about what we have been doing at the lake is more concerning because that is the result of actions we took. We no doubt deserve some additional form of discipline. Also, if he is Aegir, then why did Mother not want him to know what we are doing?

DNA Results

Jon

AS WE ALL DRIVE HOME from school, we are forced to listen to Jill talk about the lake party. She is all about it, that's for sure.

"I can't believe I am going to my first high school party. Gaddy and Ronny invited me personally after cheer practice. They said I would be their special guest of honor. Can you believe that? It took you losers how many years to get invited to your first party, and it took me less than one week."

"Actually," Marc says, "this is our first party. As far as we know, there haven't been any parties that we missed. At least, not really missed, because we wouldn't normally be interested."

I agree, "Yeah, parties aren't really our scene."

Jill mocks, "Yeah right. You keep telling yourself that. Maybe you will believe it."

"Actually, Jill, we wouldn't be going to this one if it wasn't for Darla asking. I mean, Principal Douglas was pretty clear on that today. There is no way Marc and I would disobey him. I might even talk to Mom and Dad about it."

"Don't you dare, Jon! We are going."

"Oh really? *We* are going?"

"That's right. You are going to give me a ride."

"Well, yes, my princess, it would be our honor to escort thee to the soirée."

"Whatever. I just need to get there because I promised Gaddy."

"Roger that," Marc says.

The Corolla comes to a stop, and I put it in park.

Jill jumps out and repeats, "Not a word to Mom and Dad about Principal Douglas. Promise me, Jon."

"Sure, I promise, Jill."

I mean, how big of a deal could it be? It's just a party at the lake, and we have more important things to get to with Grandpa. I never said that I wouldn't tell Grandpa about the party details, though. I'm definitely going to do that. I'll take his advice on what I should and shouldn't do about the whole thing. He's already aware because of the texts we received last night. I would have told him, anyway. Grandpa really always needs to know where I am in case the APS calls.

Speaking of the APS, Grandpa tells us he has the DNA results back from the water bottle.

"Did they get enough DNA from the water, Grandpa?"

"Oh, there was plenty in the water, all right."

"What does that mean?"

"Well, the DNA results came back negative for gods or giants. There was a good mix, probably built up over the week and augmented by backwash and the fingerprints of dozens of football players. Jon, did you do anything special to prepare the bottle before giving it to them?"

"What do you mean by *special*?"

"Did you say any Bragi rhymes or use magic of any kind on it?"

"No. Should I have done that? I wouldn't have even thought of doing something like that."

"Okay, well, we didn't find any DNA, but we did find magic swirling around in the bottle. It was absorbed into the water. We do not see that often, so we needed to rule you out."

"Well, I definitely didn't use any magic. I, for sure, wouldn't do that without talking to you first. I'm more careful than that."

I remember the incident with the egg, though, and feel a bit of guilt for withholding that from Grandpa. It's not like I would get in a lot of trouble, but I know I am not supposed to use my magic in a way that could be discovered by humans or any other type of being that may be watching.

"Good, that's good, Jon. We have really only seen this type of thing once before, and that was far away from here. About fifty years ago, the APS encountered a group in South America who were descendants of Aegir and Ran."

"The god and goddess of the sea?"

"Well, they were sea giants. At least Aegir was, and Ran was descended from a god. They were known for throwing wild parties. In fact, they got so bad at one point that Odin had to step in and put an end to them. We don't know everything that he did because it isn't recorded, but we know that the parties stopped, and Aegir and Ran split up. They resurface every now and again as their descendants are drawn to each other. They really can't help it. We don't know exactly why or how it happens, but it happens every generation. We suspect some sort of a curse separates them and then brings them back together, but it's really hard to say with Odin. He is capable of anything."

"So, it might be possible that Sam is a descendant of Aegir? He's friendly and endearing, quite the gracious host, and everybody loves him. That could make sense, right?"

Grandpa nods. "Yes, that would make sense. If he is who we think he is, it could be okay since he has a good reputation amongst Asgardians. But if Aegir's descendants are drawn together again, it could mean trouble if Ran's influence resurfaces."

Marc starts to speak up, but I plead with him with my eyes not to do it.

I pull him aside and tell him, "Let's just try to confirm it ourselves at the lake party."

"Yeah, let's do that," Marc agrees.

Grandpa then shifts the conversation. "Tonight, I want to work on something different. Instead of guiding a mouse through a maze, I want you to change your approach. Have the mouse ask the questions as to where to go."

This is a new twist on our usual training, and I am intrigued. I focus on the mouse, sensing its fear and hunger. It's a tiny creature in a confusing place, just wanting to find its way to the cheese at the end of the maze.

"Okay, little guy," I whisper a rhyme:
> "Little one, in this maze so tight,
> Share your worries, I'll be your light.
> Speak your mind, I'll guide you clear,
> To the end, away from here."

The mouse's thoughts come to me in a rush. It's scared and just wants to get out of the maze. I guide it with gentle nudges, letting it find its own way. The process is slow at first, but as we continue, the mouse becomes more confident. It's a strange but enlightening experience, teaching me more about clear communication than I expected.

After the session, I feel a deeper connection to him.

Grandpa seems pleased with the progress, nodding approvingly. "Good job, Jon. This kind of training is crucial. It helps you understand the perspectives of other animals, which is essential for a Bragi."

Marc and I head back upstairs, our minds buzzing with everything we learned.

As we get ready to leave, Marc's phone buzzes again.

"Hey, we got another text from Taylor about the party. Looks like it's going to be even bigger than we thought."

I nod. "Yeah, I've been getting texts, too. I guess everyone is talking about it."

Marc grins. "You know, Jon, this could be our chance to really figure out what's going on with Sam. If he is a descendant of Aegir, we need to know. You know, ever since reading the *Jotnar Myths* in class though, I have wondered about Darla's cousins. What if they are somehow involved in this? Maybe with Sam?"

"Yeah, I don't know. Something about that doesn't seem right to me. I just can't imagine Sam doing anything that would put anyone in harm's way. It just doesn't feel like him to me."

"Maybe it's like Grandpa said. Maybe some girl is going to get to him and that will lead him down a different path. Do any of Darla's cousins seem interested in Sam?"

"Well, I think every girl in the school is interested in Sam. Just look at him. However, I am really stuck thinking about that wolf we saw. How is that possibly related to all of this? That's what I would like to know."

"Well, gods and giants are known to shift shapes, as well, Jon. We have definitely seen that before, and Grandpa has talked about it, too."

"That's true. Well, let's see if I get visited by the wolf again in a dream tonight. Maybe he will shed some light on all of this."

"Maybe. We'll know soon enough."

Dad Talk

Darla

AS DAD AND I WALK ON the paths through the fields on our farm, I can tell he's deep in thought.

The late afternoon sun filters through the trees, casting shadows on the ground. The air is cooling down from the heat of the day and filled with the scent of pine and earth. The familiar sound of our footsteps crunching on the field is oddly comforting, but I'm still a bit shocked and a bit ticked off.

"Darlin', I never really meant to keep this from you," Dad begins, breaking the silence. "To be honest, I never thought your mother would be able to find all of them. It truly is impressive that she was able to pull that off."

I look at him, confused. "What do you mean, Dad?"

He sighs and stops walking, turning to face me. "Before you were born, both your mother and I were searching the world, trying to find descendants of the daughters of the waves. Your mother did all kinds of terrible things. Whenever she thought she found one, she would try to convince them to come with us. If they refused, she would capture them. The reality is that, most of the time, she was wrong, and she was putting kids through all of these terrible things without getting anything out of it. I tried everything I could to stop her, but only you could do that, darlin'."

I feel a lump in my throat. "*Me?*"

"Yep, everything changed when you were born," he says softly. "All of a sudden, nothing meant more to me in the entire world than protecting you and providing you with a stable home to grow up in. I made your mother promise to stop what she was doing and allow you to grow up. That might be a little bit why she is so tough on you and sometimes seems to resent you. I'm sorry for that, darlin'."

We start walking again, the path taking us deeper into the fields.

"Your mother can be quite intimidating to almost everyone, including me," he continues. "I'll do my best to contain her, but now that the nine daughters of the waves are assembled, that will be much more difficult."

I nod, processing everything he's telling me.

He stops again, his face serious. "I need to have a conversation with you about what really happened at scout camp this summer. I know it was more than what you let on. There's no way you wandered off on your own like everyone said, and you certainly didn't get lost in the woods."

I take a deep breath and reluctantly describe the whole story. "The Lokis kidnapped me, Dad. If it hadn't been for a Bragi, I might not have made it out alive."

His eyes widen in shock and anger. "A Loki? Some descendants of Loki kidnapped you?"

I nod. "They were trying to get to the Bragi who actually kind of killed them while trying to save his friend. I don't really know all the details of that, but they were angry and were taking it out on me. I don't know what they would have done if that Bragi hadn't saved me. After we defeated them and escaped, a bunch of people, who looked like police, came and talked to every camper, basically brainwashing them into telling the story about me wandering off and getting lost."

Dad's face turns red with rage. "How dare they? How dare they kidnap my daughter? I swear I'll deal with those terrible Loki descendants. They will pay for this. I don't know how, but I will find a way."

I've never seen him so worked up before. It's both scary and touching to see how much he loves me and how he can't imagine anything bad happening to me. I know he means it.

"Dad, it's okay. The Bragi saved me and sent the Lokis to Hades or somewhere, because they vanished. That's all I know."

"I would like to meet this Bragi and thank him properly."

"There's more, Dad," I say hesitantly. "The Bragi ... he's someone I like. I think I like him a lot. His name is Jon Bragg, and I invited him to the party."

Dad's expression softens a bit. "Interesting. Well, it's not entirely uncommon for giants and gods to feel an attraction to each other. How does he feel about you?"

"I think he likes me, too," I admit, blushing slightly.

Just then, we hear a noise in the bushes.

Dad stiffens and motions for me to be quiet. We hear the noise again, followed by a soft laugh. Dad's face hardens as he commands, "Air, appear Himinglaeva."

The air shimmers, and we see Liv running back toward the house.

Dad sighs deeply. "This is not good."

"Why would Mother want to gather all the daughters of the waves?" I ask.

"A long time ago, our ancestors would throw lavish parties where gods and giants gathered. They started getting out of hand, probably because of too much drinking and definitely because of too many egos in one place. Odin first tried to restore order to the parties by protecting our domain, rendering every giant or god powerless when in our realm. This worked for a while, but the gods and giants just took their party disputes elsewhere. Finally, Odin ordered Loki to seal off our realm. Loki did that, but Ran made a deal with him."

He pauses to see if I'm okay and still following along. Then Dad's face darkens. "There's a family legend that says, to break the spells Odin and Loki placed on Aegir and Ran's domain, all of their descendants must come together. It takes the whole family, and they have to all meet in a special place. You see, all doors to our world below the sea were sealed except one. It took us years to find it. It's right here at Harmony Grove, in the middle of the lake. We can enter there, offer a human sacrifice, and then return to our realm below the seas, coming and going as we please again."

My heart sinks. "Wait! A human sacrifice?"

"Yes," Dad says grimly. "I've been resisting going to Harmony Grove because I know what is required. Your mother's determination to gather the daughters of the waves means she's planning to break the spell."

We reach a clearing in the woods, and Dad stops, turning to face me. "Darlin', I need you to understand how serious this is. We're dealing with forces that are much bigger than us. But no matter what happens, I will always protect you."

Tears well up in my eyes as I nod. "I understand, Dad. I'll do whatever it takes to help."

He pulls me into a hug, holding me tightly. "We'll get through this, darlin'. Together."

As we stand there, I hear a distant rustling in the trees. I pull back from Dad and look around, but I don't see anything. "What was that?"

Dad's eyes narrow. "Stay close, darlin'. We need to be careful."

We make our way back to the house, the weight of our conversation hanging heavy in the air. As we approach, I see Liv standing near the edge of the woods, watching us with a curious expression.

"Liv, what are you doing out here?" Dad asks sternly.

She shrugs, trying to look nonchalant. "Just getting some fresh air."

Dad narrows his eyes. "I gave you an order. Do you not know how to follow orders? I know you are young, but you need to respect your elders."

Liv nods, looking a bit chastened. "I'm sorry, Aegir. I won't do it again."

"Good," he says firmly. "Now go inside and help Mother"

As Liv runs back to the house, Dad turns to me. "You know what? Let's go check the fence line. I'm not quite ready to deal with what is waiting inside."

We continue our walk, the tension left behind at the house. Dad starts telling me about one of the wildest parties Aegir and Ran ever threw for the gods, a night to remember, for sure.

"It was one of our legendary feasts," Dad begins. "Aegir and Ran had invited all the gods to our underwater hall, which was glittering with gold and pearls. The mead was flowing freely, and everyone was in high spirits. Loki, always the trickster, decided it would be a good idea to challenge Thor to a drinking contest."

I could already see where this was going. "Oh no, that sounds like a disaster waiting to happen."

Dad chuckles. "You have no idea. Thor, never one to back down from a challenge, accepted immediately. The two of them went at it, gulping down horn after horn of mead. The other gods cheered them on, and the atmosphere grew more raucous by the minute. Eventually, things got heated. Loki, always pushing boundaries, started mocking Thor, saying he couldn't handle his drink. Thor, being Thor, responded by throwing a goblet at Loki's head."

I can't help but laugh at the mental image. "And I bet Loki didn't take that well."

"Not at all," Dad continues. "Loki retaliated by summoning a storm inside the hall. Thunder roared, and lightning cracked through the water. Tables were overturned, and gods and goddesses scrambled to avoid getting caught in the chaos. In the middle of it all, Thor grabbed his hammer, Mjölnir, and swung it at Loki. Loki dodged, but the hammer hit one of Odin's prized relics—the Crystal of Eternity. It shattered into a thousand pieces."

"Wow," I say, wide-eyed. "Odin must have been furious."

"Furious doesn't even begin to cover it," Dad replies, shaking his head. "He stormed into the hall, bellowing for order. The room fell silent, except for the sound of the storm Loki had conjured still raging in the background. Odin looked at the shattered crystal, his face growing darker with every passing second. He turned to Thor and Loki, his eyes blazing with anger. In a voice that shook the very foundations of Aegir's hall, he declared that they had brought shame upon the gods with their childish behavior."

I nod, absorbing the story. "I guess even gods need to learn their limits. But why does there need to be a human sacrifice?" I ask, still struggling to wrap my head around it. "Why would that be a requirement?"

"You see, the spell Odin created just prevented magic; it really was the giants that sealed the entrances to our realm that are requiring the sacrifice. Of course, Loki was the main giant behind everything, and he made a deal with Ran.

"Loki has always enjoyed a good game. He scattered the daughters of the waves, closed all but one portal to our realm, and told her what it would take to get them opened back up. She had to find all the daughters, congregate at the one portal, and offer up the sacrifice. If she did all of that, then Loki would take care of the rest."

We walk in silence for a while, the gravity of the situation sinking in. I realize just how much my parents have been hiding from me, and how much danger we're all in.

"Dad, what are we going to do?" I ask, feeling a mix of fear and determination.

"We're going to find a way to stop this," he says firmly. "We'll protect our family and prevent any harm from coming to you or anyone else who you know."

We reach the edge of the field and pause, looking out at our home. The sun is almost set, casting a warm glow over the landscape. It's a moment of calm before the storm, and I take a deep breath, steeling myself for the challenges ahead.

"Let's go inside," Dad says, putting a reassuring hand on my shoulder. "The most important thing is that all of us should not go to Harmony Grove together. I intend to stay away from this party, that's for sure."

Oh Sister

Jon

BECAUSE WE AGREED NOT to talk to Mom and Dad, I have to come up with an excuse to bring something to the lake party that would make sense to Mom. I decide that the best approach would be to make it as close to true as possible.

"Hey, Mom, is it okay if I bake some cookies to take over to Darla?" I ask, trying to sound casual.

"Well, I don't know, Jon. Do you know how to bake cookies?" she replies, looking at me with a mix of surprise and skepticism.

"Yeah, Mrs. Dunham showed us how in home economics this week. I can do it, Mom," I assure her, trying to sound confident.

"Okay then, but only if I can watch and talk with you."

"Sure, Mom, that would be great."

I pull out my notebook because I wrote down the recipe we used in class. It's not too crazy, and I don't need to make a ton of them because everyone will probably be bringing something or, at least, I assume they will be.

Mom glances over the recipe then starts pointing me in the right direction to gather the ingredients. Sometimes, she just grabs the next item because it's easier than trying to tell me where things like vanilla extract are in the pantry.

"Here's what you need," she says, handing me the vanilla extract.

"Thanks, Mom. This is going to be fun."

We get everything set up on the kitchen counter—the solid vegetable shortening, light brown sugar, white granulated sugar, eggs, vanilla extract, water, flour, baking soda, salt, and semi-sweet chocolate chips. Mom has already read ahead and turned on the oven to preheat it to 375°F degrees.

"Mom, how did you know that Dad was the one for you?" I ask, trying to keep the conversation going.

"Well, we started dating when we were about your age. We kind of grew up together. Dad was just a goofball, but he was my goofball. We just enjoyed doing things together, like homecoming dances, proms, and everything in-between. Before I knew it, I just couldn't imagine life without him. It just felt right. I'm not sure how to explain it," she says, a nostalgic smile on her face.

"I think I understand. When I am with Darla, I know I would do anything for her. Does that sound weird?" I ask, focusing on mixing the shortening and sugars.

"No, Jon, that sounds normal. Do you know how she feels about you?" Mom asks, genuinely interested.

"I think she likes me, too," I say, feeling a bit shy about admitting it.

Next, I add in the eggs, vanilla extract, and water, making the mixture creamy and until it's light in color and fluffy in texture. In a separate bowl, I whisk together the flour, baking soda, and salt to remove all lumps.

"That's nice. I'm happy for you. Darla always seemed like a nice girl at dance competitions," Mom says, watching me work.

"Thanks, Mom. She is really special," I say, carefully folding the flour-coated chocolate chips into the dough.

"You want to avoid large chunks of flour. Really, chunks of anything. Nobody wants a big bite of flour in their mouth," Mom says, stepping in to help mix the dough better. She makes it look so easy as she folds it over and over, mixing things up until the dough is perfect.

I drop teaspoon-sized amounts onto the parchment-lined baking sheets then put them in the preheated oven for exactly twelve minutes.

As the cookies bake, Mom and I chat more.

"It's nice of you to do this for her. I'm sure she will appreciate it. It's always nice to do something with your own hands for the people you love. It's one of the reasons why I like cooking for all of you so much," she says, smiling warmly.

"You're the best, Mom. Thanks for helping," I say, feeling grateful.

"Don't mention it, Jonboy. Happy to spend time with you. Now, let's clean up this mess we made," she says, rolling up her sleeves.

We make short work of the cleanup tasks, and by the time the cookies are done, everything is back where it belongs. The bowls, spoons, whisks, and measuring spoons are nestled into the dishwasher.

"Darla is a lucky girl," Mom says, looking at the cooling cookies.

"Well, I'm a lucky guy to have a great mom like you. Thanks for the help and for the talk You're the best," I say, giving her a hug.

"You're welcome, Jonboy. I'm going to go take care of some laundry. Be sure to let those cookies cool before putting them into a container," she says, heading out of the kitchen.

"I will, Mom. Thanks again," I call after her.

As I'm putting the cookies into a container, Jill walks into the kitchen. "What were you and Mom talking about?" she demands, folding her arms.

"Nothing. Relax, Jill. I didn't say anything about your precious party." I roll my eyes.

"You better not have! I wouldn't want to have to tell Jess, Gaddy, and Ronny that you ruined it for us." She glares at me.

"Jill, please. Mom was just helping me with the cookies. I want to bring something tonight, and since we aren't telling Mom, this was the best thing I could think of right now," I explain, trying to keep my cool.

She seems satisfied with that ... for now, turning her back and walking back up the stairs to her room. No doubt to text somebody something "extremely important," like what they are going to wear to the party today or some other girl stuff.

I head downstairs to study up on some rhymes. I want to be as prepared as I can be.

I snap a few pictures of water manipulation rhymes and protection spells from my notebook. After all, I'm still a good scout, and Harmony Grove brings back too many memories. I need to be careful.

Then I remember that I have no idea where my swimming trunks are because I wear them so infrequently. I need to find Mom.

"Mom, do you know where my swimming trunks are?" I ask, walking into the laundry room.

"Why? You never go swimming," she says, looking up from folding clothes.

"Well, Darla and her family invited some of us to go swim at the lake," I explain as best I can without bringing up the word *party*.

"Oh, how nice. Your swimming trunks are in the bottom drawer of your dresser, toward the right back of the drawer. The back of your bottom drawer is where I put all of the clothes you rarely wear," she says with a knowing smile.

"Thanks, Mom. What would I do without you?" I say, grateful for her organizational skills.

"You definitely wouldn't be swimming in your swim trunks," she replies with a laugh.

I run back upstairs, find my trunks exactly where she said they would be, and then head back downstairs, taking the last three steps in one big leap. As I land, I see that Jill is downstairs, ready and waiting. She's holding the container of cookies.

"Let's go, Jon. I don't want to be late," she says, tapping her foot impatiently.

"Late? Haven't you heard of being fashionably late?" I joke, trying to lighten the mood.

"Yeah, but I promised I would help Gaddy and Ronny with setting things up." She rolls her eyes.

"Okay, okay. Let's go swing by and pick up Marc," I say, grabbing my keys.

I tell Mom goodbye and let her know where we're going to be and about when I plan to be home. She already knows, but that's something we do every time we go anywhere. Mom doesn't like surprises, even though she can track us on our phones. the rule is she shouldn't have to if we communicate well.

The drive to Marc's house is filled with Jill's excited chatter about the party. She's way more excited about it than I am.

"This is going to be so much fun. I can't believe Gaddy and Ronny invited me personally. They said I'd be their guest of honor," Jill gushes, practically bouncing in her seat.

I look over at her, thinking, *We already talked about this*, but then I decide to match her enthusiasm. "Yeah, neat. I'm sure it's going to be great."

When we arrive at Marc's house, he hops into the car with a grin. "Ready for this?" he asks, giving me a fist-bump.

"As ready as I'll ever be," I reply, pulling away from the curb.

We drive to the lake with Jill talking nonstop about all the things she's looking forward to at the party.

The scenery changes as we get closer to Harmony Grove, the dense forest giving way to the sparkling brownish hue of the lake. The sun casts a bright light over everything.

Teasing

Darla

I CAN'T BELIEVE THAT Liv told Mother, and I assume everyone else, what she heard from my conversation with Dad.

Mother's voice is like a thunderclap. "Darla Bara Towns! How dare you keep this from me?"

Dad jumps in, trying to defuse the situation, "Now, let's just calm down. You and I both know this is a natural thing. It's common for gods and giants to be attracted to each other, especially a son of Odin."

"Do *not* defend her!" Mother screeches, her eyes blazing with fury.

Dad keeps his tone even. "We can talk about this later. There is no need to make this worse than it needs to be for Darla right now."

"Oh, we *will* be talking about this—you can bet on that!"

"Fine. darlin', why don't you go upstairs and let your mother and I talk?"

I happily agree because I have no idea how I am going to respond to Mother.

Jon and I really haven't talked about this that much, so I think she is making a big deal out of nothing. Unfortunately, I'm sure Mother isn't the only one who is going to have something to say on the matter. I'm going to have to deal with the cousins.

As I get up to my room, I hear Mother and Dad going at it. I am sure everyone hears it for a couple of miles around because they are not keeping it down, which is not like them, not like them at all.

Mother feels betrayed because of the damage a Bragi could do to their plans. Dad is in full-on defensive mode, trying to protect me. He keeps saying, "Enough with your plan already. Why can't you just let her be a kid and have normal experiences?"

Mother says, "*Normal*? You think getting involved with a Bragi is *normal*? You have lost your mind!"

Then I hear a door slam and an uneasy silence. At least it is over.

With that, I hear a knock on my door. I already know it is Olga.

I reply, "Not now, Olga."

"Darla, let me in. We really need to talk."

Reluctantly, I let her in because I am guessing I could easily be commanded to do so, and I am done with fighting that for now.

"What? What could we possibly need to talk about?"

"We need to know that you are on our side, Darla."

"What does that mean?"

"Well, if push comes to shove at the party, can we count on you to help the family?"

"That depends on what the family is planning to do. If the family is planning on sacrificing a human, then no, you cannot count on me to help in any way with that."

"So, your father told you our history?"

"Yes, he did. Well, he told me enough."

"Did he tell you what happens when we are successful?"

"He said the doors to our world will open up around the world, and we will be able to freely pass back and forth."

"Exactly. We will be able to go to our homes—all of us—and then we can meet anytime we want in our realm. We won't have to be here, in Bluehill, with you. You can have your home back. You can be done with all of this if you want, or you can join us. Whatever you want, but it would be up to you."

I have to admit that sounds like a dream come true. I would love for this to be over. I'm tired of all of this, especially having the cousins around all the time.

"Just promise me you will think about it."

"Sure, I'll think about it, but I'm telling you there are lines I am not going to cross."

"Understood. Thanks, Darla. That's all we are asking."

With that, Olga leaves me alone, and I am stuck thinking about all of this and also concerned about what Mother is going to do. I'm also worried about Jon because now not only does my dad know, but by now, Mother *and* the cousins do. This puts him in a dangerous position of possibly being exposed. I didn't mean to do that. I told Dad because I know he can be completely trusted, but the cousins could tell anyone.

Ready to let this all go, I close my eyes for a moment and my thoughts drift away.

As I am dreaming, I am in the woods, and I encounter this huge bear. However, he seems friendly, like I have known him my whole life. The bear approaches me, and I try to remember what you are supposed to do when a bear approaches. Do I stay still? Do I play dead? I know I definitely do not run.

I decide to drop and play dead.

The bear comes over and looks down at me with his big bear nose right in my face and says, "What are you doing, Darla?"

Great, the bear is talking and isn't going to leave.

I decide to ask, "How do you know my name, bear?"

"Because I am one of your closest friends. Think, Darla."

I pause, but somehow, I immediately know.

"Sam, is that you?"

The big bear nods.

"W-what? No, how is this possible?"

"There's no time for that, Darla. What your mother and cousins are planning is dangerous. I've seen what you have been doing at Harmony Grove. You have to stop them before it's too late."

"This is bigger than me, Sam. I'm not sure I could stop them if I wanted to."

"But will you try, Darla? It's all that I ask, and I'm sure Jon will help."

"Sam, what do you know about Jon?"

"I know everything."

With that, I wake up to Mother shaking the bed to wake me.

"Get up. We have preparations to make for the party, and your father is unavailable, so you will need to step up for the family."

"Yes, Mother. But what do you mean Dad is unavailable?"

"No more questions. Let's go."

As we drive out to the lake, the other girls are relentlessly harassing me about being in love with Jon Bragg. I can barely handle it, to be honest.

"Look, you overheard something you should not have heard, and I never said I was in love with Jon Bragg. I think I *might* like him, and he might like me."

Gaddy giggles. "Why not find out tonight, sis? You know what it's like to kiss an Asgardian, right?"

"Actually, no. We aren't a PDA type of couple."

"Oh, so you are a couple then?" Ronny chimes in, her eyes sparkling with mischief.

"No, that's not what I meant."

"Well, you need to be careful with a Bragi. They can do just about anything with their words," Billow adds with a smirk.

"Yeah, that's not true. I know for a fact that the magic they use works on everyone but me. The only reason I got nabbed by that Loki was because he used chloroform to knock me out and take me away. Also, I don't know why I am talking about this with all of you. Just leave me alone, please."

"Alone with Jon Bragg, you bet," Duff says, winking.

"Great," I retort, trying to sound bolder than I feel.

AT THE LAKE, AS SOON as Jon and Marc reemerge from the woods, the cousins all make a beeline for Jon, and I do my best to intervene.

"Jon, can we please talk?" I turn to them. "In private?"

"*Ooo*," they all say in unison, "In private." Giggles ripple through the group.

"Grow up," I snap, grabbing Jon's hand and pulling him away from the group.

We walk toward a quieter part of the lake, away from the growing crowd. The air is crisp and cool, with the scent of grass and lake water. The sun is setting, casting a golden glow over the water, making it sparkle like a thousand diamonds.

"Sorry about them," I say, finally letting go of Jon's hand. "They can be a bit much."

"It's okay," Jon replies, smiling. "I'm just glad we get to spend some time together."

I feel a warmth spread through me at his words. "Me, too," I admit. "There's something I need to talk to you about."

Jon looks at me, concern etched on his face. "What is it, Darla?"

"I had a dream earlier today. A bear spoke to me. It was Sam. He warned me about the party. He said it could be dangerous."

Jon's eyes widen. "A talking bear? Are you sure it was Sam?"

"Yes, I'm sure. He said we should be careful."

Jon nods slowly. "Well, that's interesting. I have been visited by a wolf in my dreams for a few nights now. He was about as helpful as your bear and gave me a similar warning. For now, it's just a party, and we just need to stay alert."

I nod, feeling a bit more at ease. "Thanks, Jon. You're right."

"Let's just try to have some fun." he says, squeezing my hand.

As we talk, more guests arrive. The air is filled with the sounds of laughter and music, but I can't seem to enjoy it. My mind is racing with thoughts of what could happen tonight.

The cousins are welcoming the other guests, and I can see Mother overseeing everything with a watchful eye. I feel a knot in my stomach as I remember her reaction earlier. I have to be careful tonight. One wrong move, and everything could fall apart.

"Darla, are you okay?" Jon asks, noticing my unease.

"Yeah."

"Don't worry. It's just a party," he reassures me.

The Confession

Jon

I CAN'T BELIEVE THAT Darla had a dream about Sam, as well. That has to mean something. However, I wonder why he chose to take bear form with her versus the wolf form with me. It's something I'll need to ask him.

Earlier, when Marc, Jill, and I arrived, Marc and I headed out to the woods to track the wolf. It was a long shot, but we knew we had to try. It wasn't difficult to find him, either, because he was, in fact, waiting for us, with a message he wanted to deliver.

I used a rhyme to allow him to talk to me.

"Oh, great wolf that is standing there,
I can see how much you really do care.
Please feel free to talk to me now,
As I am quite sure that you know how."

With that, Sam identified himself and started talking freely. Apparently, when we are asleep, he can enter our dreams and communicate with us. He already knew about me, and that is why he was being protective of me at school—he knew I was Bragi. That is a gift that skinwalkers have—they can see the nature of a being. It's also why he is not so impressed by Brad Dillon. He can see that Brad has a lot of ugly internal thoughts.

Sam told me about what he saw at the lake recently with the dead fish, mist, and other strange things. He was in the process

180

of describing who he saw when we were interrupted by someone coming. It was Darla and her cousins.

As Darla and I walk for a bit in silence, just being together, we eventually make our way over to an empty spot to sit in front of the fire. I look over to Marc and then at Jill. I motion for him to head over, and he nods, knowing exactly what I want him to do—keep an eye on my sister. I can tell Darla has something she is struggling to find the words to say to me.

The party is under way by the time we settle by the fire. There's a sand volleyball game starting, and Darla's cousins are playing. They are really quite good, and a crowd has gathered to watch them. The atmosphere is buzzing with screams of excitement with each volley.

By the shore, people are paddling around in canoes, their laughter echoing over the water. There are also paddle boats for those who prefer more leisurely water transportation. Several people are swimming in the lake, some jumping off rocks and into the deep water, or swinging from a tire swing into the lake. The splash and shouts of joy add to the festive atmosphere.

The air is filled with the mouthwatering aroma of grilled hot dogs and burgers. Some of the football guys are manning the grills at the request of Mrs. Towns and the cousins. It's clear those girls have them wrapped around their fingers. Plates piled high with food are being passed around, and everyone seems to be enjoying themselves.

As we sit next to each other, I can almost see a glow coming off Darla. She looks so beautiful. I have never seen her look so ... radiant. Is she smiling?

I manage to smile back and say, "See? It's all going to be fine."

She looks at me, her smile fading slightly. "Lately, any time I am around water, I just feel different."

"How so?" I ask, genuinely curious.

"Jon, I need to tell you something." She seems almost afraid to speak.

"Whatever you have to say, it couldn't possibly be worse than what we have already been through, right?"

She leans in and whispers, "You know the poem we read in English class about the daughters of the nine waves?"

"Yes, of course I do."

"Well, that's me and my cousins. We are the descendants of the nine daughters, and my mother is a descendant of Ran. I just found out that my father is a descendant of Aegir."

Somehow, I knew that was true all along.

"I was kind of hoping it wasn't you, but the APS is aware of some giants in the area and, well, they are on to you. They know that the giants are descendants of Aegir and Ran. In fact, we thought that Sam might be Aegir."

"On to us? The APS is on to us? Wait—Sam?"

"Yes," I whisper back. "Of course, now we know that Sam is a skinwalker."

Darla looks at me, wide-eyed. "What? That's a real thing, too? The bear in my dream was really him?"

I nod affirmatively and start to explain the history of what we know about skinwalkers.

As we are talking, Darla's cousin, Gaddy, comes over, her face lit with mischief and trouble. "So, I hear you are a Brag ... gard," Gaddy says loudly, drawing the attention of several nearby partygoers.

My eyes are huge, as I thought she was going to say it for everyone to hear.

Darla mouths, "*Sorry*."

I reply, "Well, sorry, Gaddy, but you heard wrong. I've got absolutely nothing to brag about and never have."

Gaddy persists, "That's not what I heard."

I feel a bunch of eyes land on us as this drama unfolds, but I try again to distract away from this conversation. "It's a great party. Thanks for doing this."

Gaddy doesn't back down. "Don't try to change the subject."

Darla steps in, her voice strong and clear. "Leave him alone. Go find Mother."

Shockingly, Gaddy turns around and walks in the other direction.

"Nothing to see here, folks. Go about your business," I tell the others.

Darla and I return to our conversation, but the moment has been tainted by the interruption. I feel the weight of what she just disclosed pressing down on me, and an even greater weight around the fact that Gaddy seems to know my secret.

We watch as the volleyball game continues, the cousins dominating the court. The crowd cheers them on, their energy infectious. The sun has set, and the sky is now a deep blue, with the first stars starting to twinkle overhead. The lake reflects the moonlight, creating a serene and almost magical atmosphere.

"Jon, I'm sorry about Gaddy. I was talking to my dad in private, and Liv overheard what we were talking about, which was you. Dad asked me what really happened at scout camp, and I told him everything, thinking we were alone. Liv ran back and told all of my cousins. I'm so sorry, but I don't know what they are going to do now that they know."

"I know how much you trust your dad, and I know you didn't mean for them to find out about me. Let's just do our best to keep the damage to a minimum tonight, and I'll talk to Grandpa to see if there is a way to fix this for us long-term."

As we sit there, the sounds of the party around us start to fade into the background. I can't help but feel that this moment, right here and now, is a turning point. We are being honest about who we are, and it is drawing us closer.

Darla explains how their hive mentality works, how they can hear each other and command each other when they want, which is how she ordered Gaddy away. I wonder if the APS is aware of that.

The night wears on, and the party shows no signs of slowing down. The cousins are now challenging some of the football guys to tug-of-war. The guys are confident, but it's clear the cousins are stronger than they look, which makes sense now.

The crowd gathers around, cheering and laughing as the contest begins. The rope strains under the pressure and, for a moment, it looks like the football guys might have the upper hand. But then, with a burst of strength, the cousins pull them across the line, winning the match. The crowd erupts in cheers, and the football guys, though good-natured about their loss, look a bit bewildered.

I watch Darla laugh at the scene, and I can't help but smile. Despite everything, she still has moments of joy. Moments that remind me to enjoy the good times while we can, as anything can happen.

As the night deepens, the fire pit becomes the center of attention. People gather around, roasting marshmallows and telling stories. The flickering flames cast long shadows, creating an intimate and almost surreal atmosphere.

Marc joins us by the fire, bringing over a plate of cookies he managed to snag from the food table. "Here, thought you might want some of these."

"Thanks, Marc," I say, taking a cookie and handing one to Darla. "How's Jill doing?"

Marc chuckles. "She's having a blast. I think she's convinced half the school to be her new best friend."

"Sounds like her," I say, smiling.

Lights Out

Darla

I DID IT. I CANNOT believe I finally told Jon.

We have been sitting here for a while now, just watching for any sign of trouble. Mostly in silence but staying fully aware. The night is cool, and I shiver slightly. As if he can sense it, Jon gets a little closer and puts his arm behind me. It feels good. As he leans toward me, I look into his eyes and brace myself for what is coming. Then, just as his lips are about to touch mine, we hear a scream coming from the crowd.

We both jerk back and look toward the source of the noise. The water has engulfed the party, and everyone is struggling to run out of the water. The serene lake has turned into a chaotic mess. We see one girl being pulled back in as if the current is too strong for her.

I glance all around, looking for my sisters—I mean, cousins—and see them with their hands clasped and a look of pure determination on their faces.

"What are they doing?" I mutter, half to myself.

Jon and I run over to them, but before we can reach them, my mother appears. A loud thunderclap echoes through the night as she slams her hands together and, once again, the world goes black.

"What are they doing? Why are they doing it without me? Can they do it without Dad and me? I thought they needed us. Dad isn't here," I argue with myself, even as I feel I am unconscious.

Suddenly, I see a wolf coming toward me.

Is this what Jon was talking about?

He is huge, but I can see in his eyes that he is not looking to hurt me. He is rather concerned for me.

"Darla, are you okay?" The voice is familiar, almost comforting.

"Sam, is that you?"

"Yes, Darla, it's me. I am beside you and Jon. We need you to wake up first. You are touching the water now. Can you feel it?"

I nod. "Yes, I can feel it."

"We need you to draw power from it and wake yourself up. Can you do that?"

"Yes, I think I can."

"Good, keep trying. Jon is out right now and won't have his power, as the protection spell from Odin has kicked in, and no gods are able to use their magic right now. Jon needs you to wake him up."

"Jon needs me?"

"Yes, Darla, Jon needs you. We all need you."

I suddenly feel that everyone is sleeping. The water is telling me what is happening. I can feel the fear that everyone felt when the water came upon them, as well. They were panicking when it hit, but they are still breathing, although some are covered in water. I need to wake up now.

I think to myself, "Darla Bara Towns, you *wake up!*"

With that, I open my eyes and get to my feet. I command the water to recede so that none of the partygoers are covered anymore. That's when I see Sam has joined us, but not in wolf form. He is trying to wake up Jon by nudging him. Nothing seems to be working.

As the water recedes to its banks, people start to wake up. Now they are screaming about the water being dangerous and all start running for their cars in disbelief of what happened, having no desire to stick around and see what is going to happen next.

They are moving so quickly that they leave everything behind—beach balls and wet towels left everywhere. It's amazing how fast it becomes a deserted beach.

I turn my attention to Jon, and as the water recedes past him, he awakens, jumps to his feet, and screams, "Jill! They took Jill!"

"I saw a girl out there with them. Are you sure it was Jill?"

Marc comes running over. "I'm sorry, Jon. There was nothing I could do."

"It's okay, Marc. There was nothing any of us could have done. I have to go after her."

Jon starts a rhyme:

> "Water, please help me to find,
> My sister who was taken from me.
> She was taken by your embrace,
> Tell me where she happens to be."

Nothing happens.

Jon looks around in disbelief. "Nothing happened. I can't see anything. What's wrong with me? Did they do something to me?"

I remember. Sam reminded me that Odin put a spell in place.

Sam confirms, "Yes, it is what I feared. This means that gods and giants have lost their powers and only Aegir, Ran, and the nine daughters of the waves have power here. If we leave Harmony Grove, we will feel our powers come back, but these grounds are now off-limits for us as Ran has started the ceremony and restored the rule of law in her domain."

"But why did they take my sister? She will die underwater. She has been underwater for minutes already."

"Actually, she will be fine under the water, Jon. She isn't struggling, as she has entered our realm below. She can breathe because it is below the water. Mother and my cousins need her alive … for now."

"What do you mean, *for now*?"

"Well, they need a human for the sacrifice."

"Wait—what sacrifice?"

"In order to permanently restore our realm and open up all of the portals to it, my family must all gather around the sole remaining portal, which is here at Harmony Grove. Many years ago, it was determined that our parties had gotten out of hand, and Odin took actions to stop them. Then Loki extended that by blocking all portals to our realm except one. He didn't tell Ran where it was. It took years to find the opening as location after location was scouted. The last place anyone would have expected it was a small lake in rural Iowa. Loki hid it well. Being Loki, he left open the possibility for us to remove the barriers to our realm, but it requires all of us to be present and a human sacrifice. That's why Mother threw the party—to get us here and to sacrifice a human. They know Jill is human because they know you are Bragi. I told Dad because I knew I could trust him, but Liv overheard and told Mother and the cousins. This is all happening because of me."

"Darla, it's not your fault," Jon says. "This is on your mother and cousins. However, I am confused. Did you say that your dad has to be present, as well?"

"Yes, that is what we were told."

"Okay, so where is your dad? I didn't see him out there with them. I haven't seen him all night."

"I'm willing to bet he is here," Sam says. "I also cannot feel him, nor can I shift into another form right now. If I could, then I would definitely find him quickly—my senses are always heightened in animal form. However, my powers came through Odin, so I am also unable to use them here."

"I'll see if the water will help us find him. It's possible they already took him there, too. Although I don't know how. He is quite powerful and has the ability to tell all of us what to do, even Mother. At least, he could at home."

Sam says, "If he is here, he will also have power, just like you do, Darla."

As the last of the fleeing students vanish into the distance, the silence that settles over the lake is eerie and unsettling. The moon hangs high above us, casting an otherworldly glow on the now-deserted beach. The sound of the water lapping gently against the shore is the only thing breaking the stillness.

I look at Jon, whose face is etched with determination and worry.

"We need to find your dad, Darla," Marc says, his voice steady but urgent. "If he's the key to stopping this, we can't waste any more time."

"Marc, you need to go get Grandpa," Jon tells him. "He will know what to do."

"Roger that. If anything else comes up, text me."

"We will. Just get Grandpa and tell him to contact the APS, as this is an emergency."

I nod, trying to push down the rising panic. "I'll see what I can do, too."

Kneeling by the edge of the lake, I place my hands in the cool water. Closing my eyes, I reach out with my mind, trying to connect with the essence of the water, to feel its currents and listen to its secrets. It's a strange sensation, like tuning into a frequency that's always been there but I've never noticed before.

The water speaks to me in ripples and waves, showing me glimpses of what lies beneath its surface. I see flashes of my cousins, their faces twisted in concentration as they channel their powers. I see my mother, her expression one of fierce focus. But I don't see my father.

"Darla," Sam says softly, kneeling beside me, "can you sense him?"

"I'm trying," I whisper, frustration tinging my voice. "I can see everyone else, but not him."

Jon places a reassuring hand on my shoulder. "Keep trying. You're doing great."

The encouragement helps, and I take a deep breath, focusing harder.

The images in the water start to shift and change, showing me different parts of the lake, different faces. And then, there he is. My father, bound and unconscious, lying at the bottom of the lake, surrounded by shimmering water that seems to pulse with a strange energy.

"I found him," I say, my voice trembling. "He's at the bottom of the lake. They've bound him somehow, but he is in a protective pocket of some sort. I think he created it."

Young Love

Jon

SAM'S EYES WIDEN. "WE need to get him out of there."

"But how?" Darla asks, panic rising in her voice. "I can't swim down there and free him. The water's too deep."

I squeeze her shoulder, trying to convey some sense of calm. "We'll figure it out. We have to."

Sam stands up, looking around. "We need something to break through whatever is binding him. Do you have anything sharp?"

Darla shakes her head, looking helpless. "No, nothing."

An idea starts forming in my mind. "Maybe we can use the water itself. Darla, can you control it enough to free him? I guess we don't even know what may be holding him in place. It could be magic, or it could be actual bindings."

She hesitates. "I've never tried anything like that before."

"You can do it," I tell her firmly, hoping to instill confidence. "I believe in you."

Taking a deep breath, she closes her eyes and focuses on the water. I watch as her face scrunches in concentration, her hands hovering just above the surface. I can almost feel the energy radiating from her as she connects with the water.

"Come on, Darla," she whispers to herself. "You can do this. Dad needs you."

The water begins to respond, swirling around her fingers. It's mesmerizing, watching the liquid bend to her will, forming a sharp, thin blade. She directs it downward, probably visualizing it slicing through the ties binding her father.

"There!" she gasps, opening her eyes. "I think I did it."

Sam and I exchange a hopeful glance.

"Now we just need to get him up here," Sam says.

I nod. "Let's go."

We move quickly toward the spot where Darla saw her father. The water is brownish gray but clear and cold as we wade in deeper and deeper. I can feel a current pulling us forward, almost as if it's trying to help.

Darla's focus is intense, her eyes locked on the spot where her father lies beneath the surface. She extends her hands, palms down, and I can see the strain on her face as she concentrates.

Slowly, almost imperceptibly, I see a shape rising from the depths and moving toward us. It's an agonizingly slow process, and Darla seems to be in pain, but she doesn't stop. She can't stop.

"Almost there," I encourage, my eyes never leaving her father's form.

Finally, with a final surge, her father breaks the surface, reaching for air.

Sam and I grab him, pulling him to the shore. Darla collapses onto the sand, tired but relieved.

"You did it!" I say, my voice filled with awe and respect.

Darla's father coughs, sputtering a bit as he takes in air. "Thank you," he manages to say, looking at all of us and getting his bearings.

"We need to get him out of here," Sam says urgently. "This place isn't safe."

As we help Darla's father to his feet, I look around at the now-quiet lake. I gaze out into the direction of where I last saw Jill. It has been so long, and it makes my heart ache that I cannot help her.

"Darlin'," her father says, "I'm so proud of you. That had to be difficult."

"Dad, what happened?" Darla asks, her voice trembling with emotion.

He takes a deep breath, steadying himself. "Your mother ... she tricked me. We had an argument over coffee about you and the sacrifice she was planning. I refused to participate. She wasn't happy with that, so she used an herb known as Aethervine. It's known to paralyze gods and giants. She mixed it into my coffee. I felt its effects almost immediately, but it was too late."

Aethervine, I think, recalling the stories. It is an herb the APS used in ancient times to incapacitate rogue Asgardians, making them vulnerable. The effects are potent and can last for hours, rendering even the mightiest giants immobile. I didn't even know it's still around. The herb is believed to originate from a rare plant that grows in the deep forests of Scandinavia. It's definitely not something you can get here in Grinwell.

"She is more prepared than a boy scout. She always knew it was possible she would need to incapacitate one of us," he continues. "So, she did what she thought she had to do. I'm so sorry, darlin'. I never wanted you to be involved in any of this. I'm sorry all of you kids are going through this because of my family."

"It's not your fault, Dad," Darla says, her voice firm despite the quiver. "We'll figure this out together. Should we leave? Will that stop everything? They need us here, right?"

Her dad sternly says, "No. We have to save the girl. We can't leave now. Your mother is far enough into the ceremony that she no longer needs our cooperation."

I step forward, the urgency of the situation pressing down on me. "Then we need to focus on getting Jill back. What will we need? What are the risks we are taking?"

Her father looks at me, his eyes filled with a mix of respect and shared concern. "The first thing we need to do is find out where in our realm they have taken her. If they're planning a sacrifice, they'll need to prepare. That gives us a little time, but not much. The biggest risk is that we might walk into a trap. Ran is cunning, and she'll be expecting us."

Sam nods. "We need a plan. We can't just rush in without knowing what we're up against."

I agree. "What do you suggest, Mr. Towns?"

Mr. Towns says, "First, let me tell you more about our realm. Darla and I will be able to break through any protection, and we will be able to bring one of you with us. Once we get into the outer portion of our realm, we will enter a maze that we will need to traverse. The walls shift to keep unwanted guests out during our parties, so it's never the same. There will be creatures there to block our path. Darla and I should be able to defeat them. However, it will be taxing. When we complete the maze, we will reach the inner cavern, and then we will face Ran and the other daughters of the waves, who will be rapidly gathering power."

"I am definitely going," I tell them. "It's my sister, and there has to be a way I can help."

Darla says, "You won't have your powers, Jon, so maybe we should bring Sam down with us. He's strong, and we could use his help."

"Darla, please. Mr. Towns, please. I'm begging you to take me. I will do whatever it takes to save Jill."

Mr. Towns nods. "As you wish. I have an idea as to how you might be able to help, but it's going to take more than any of us could possibly imagine. Maybe more than we are prepared to give."

"No, I can't let you go, Jon. I care too much for you. Jon, I think I love you," Darla cries.

Even in this moment, my heart starts pounding, and I look into her eyes as I realize, "I ... I love you, too, Darla."

Mr. Towns says, "Then it's settled. Jon is coming with us. There is nothing more powerful than love. Your love for each other and your love for your sister—we may be able to use that to open a tiny window of opportunity down there. You'll know when it is time, Jon. Trust your heart, and you will know what to do."

Mr. Towns turns to Sam. "We need you to find your way to the boundary of the spell so you can shift and be aware of what is happening. If we don't make it out, we may need you to warn others and explain the situation."

Sam nods, understanding the gravity of his task and accepting his role. "Yes, sir. You can count on me, but how did you know?"

Mr. Towns just looks at him and points to his heart. "Jon told Darla, and I'm sure she has told all of you, that we have a hive mentality. As soon as you told her, you told all of us."

With Sam heading off to escape the protection spell, Darla, Mr. Towns, and I quickly make preparations. We forage through the surrounding woods and camp for any makeshift weapons we can find. It's not much, but it will have to do. We gather sturdy branches, sharp stones, and even a few metal tent stakes.

The air is thick with tension as we work, the sounds of the forest around us contrasting sharply with the urgency of our task.

Mr. Towns pieces together a makeshift fishing spear. "Jon, this is the best I can do. Be careful with it."

We then hold hands, forming a circle. Mr. Towns begins to talk softly, calling upon the power of the water. The lake responds, swirling around us in a gentle yet powerful current. I can feel the pull, almost like a gentle tugging at my soul.

The water rises, lifting us. It's a strange sensation, almost like being weightless. As we descend, I can see the surface of the lake becoming more distant, the light from above dimming as we are pulled deeper into the depths. My lungs begin to burn for air, but I force myself to remain calm.

"Hold on," Mr. Towns says, his voice echoing strangely in the water. "We're almost there."

Just as I feel like I can't hold my breath any longer, we breach a barrier, and then I hear a *pop*, and we are inside something strange and unfamiliar—the maze. I gasp for air, my lungs grateful for the oxygen.

"We made it," Mr. Towns says, his voice filled with relief.

I look around, taking in our surroundings. The cavern is massive, with walls made of shimmering blue stone. The water here is crystal clear, about knee-high, and I can see strange, glowing creatures swimming in the distance.

"We need to move quickly," Mr. Towns says. "They'll know we're here soon."

We start to move through the cavern, the eerie glow of the walls lighting our way. The air is cool and damp, and the only sounds are the soft splashes of our movements and the distant hum of the creatures in the water.

"Stay close," Mr. Towns warns. "The maze can be tricky. We don't want to get separated."

I nod, gripping the spear tightly.

We move forward, the path winding and twisting in ways that make it easy to get lost. The further we go, the more I can feel the magic of this place. It's ancient and powerful, a reminder of what we're up against.

We encounter the first of the sea creatures—a massive, octopus-like beast with glowing eyes. It blocks our path, hissing menacingly.

Mr. Towns steps forward, summoning a wave of water to push the creature back. It snarls but retreats, allowing us to pass.

"Keep moving," he urges as he holds the creature in place with the water until we pass. "There will be more."

We press on, encountering more creatures as we navigate the maze. The next creature we come across is a massive, ancient fish with scales that shimmer like silver in the dim light. It glides past us, completely indifferent to our presence. Its eyes, deep and unknowable, seem to glance at us but show no interest. It's almost as if it's seen countless intruders before and knows we're not worth the trouble. The calmness of this encounter only makes me more anxious, as if it's the calm before the storm.

Our path twists and turns, and suddenly, we face a creature that Mr. Towns whispers is a Hræzla, an ancient Norse water troll. It emerges from the shadows, its body covered in seaweed and barnacles, its eyes glowing with a menacing green light. The Hræzla lets out a guttural roar, water dripping from its jagged teeth.

Darla steps forward, determination etched on her face. "Stay back," she warns us, her voice steady despite the fear I can see in her eyes.

She raises her hands, summoning the water around us. The Hræzla charges, but Darla creates a powerful wave, crashing it into the beast. It stumbles but doesn't fall. Then, with a swift motion, Darla shapes the water into a spear, hurling it at the troll. The weapon pierces its shoulder, causing it to howl in pain. Enraged, the Hræzla lunges at Darla, but she remains focused, summoning another wave to push it back. With one final effort, she creates a whirlpool, trapping the troll and dragging it away from our path.

Mr. Towns proclaims, "You're a quick learner, darlin'"

Darla looks at him then at me and shrugs. "Hive mentality."

I nod in understanding, and we press on, knowing we can't afford to stop.

The next turn reveals an even greater threat. Emerging from the depths is something I have only read about—a Marew, a monstrous sea wolf with multiple heads, each snarling and snapping at the water. Its presence exudes pure malice, and I can see Mr. Towns preparing himself for the fight.

"Stay behind me," he commands, his voice steady and strong. Then he steps forward, summoning his own command over the water. The Marew roars, each head lunging forward in a coordinated attack. Mr. Towns counters with a wall of water, blocking the beast's advance. He raises his hands, and the water around the Marew begins to freeze, trapping its legs. The creature thrashes, trying to break free, but Mr. Town's grip on the water remains firm. With a swift movement, he sends a wave of ice shards at the Marew, striking each head with precision. The beast lets out a final, agonized howl before collapsing into the water, defeated.

Panting heavily from the exertion, he turns to us and commands, "We need to keep moving. There may be more."

Each battle is taking its toll, leaving Darla and her dad more exhausted and drained. The creatures of this maze are determined to test our resolve.

Finally, we reach a clearing at the heart of the maze. At the center stands a towering archway, pulsing with a strange otherworldly light.

"That's the entrance to the real party," Mr. Towns says. "We're here."

We approach the archway, the sense of urgency growing with each step. I can feel my heart pounding in my chest, a mix of fear and determination driving me forward.

"Ready?" Mr. Towns asks, looking at both of us.

I nod, gripping the spear tightly again. "Let's do this."

With a deep breath, we step through the archway.

The Cavern

Darla

AS WE STEP THROUGH, we enter a hallway, and I immediately sense Mother and the cousins. The power they have is stronger than ever.

I turn to look at Dad, and I can see he feels it, too.

Then we hear her say, "Bragi, son of Odin, welcome to our celebration. I'd tell you to behave yourself, but as you know by now, your powers are not active here by the order of your father, Odin. Aegir and Bara, thank you for joining us. Now, bring your Bragi to me."

Dad and I grab hold of Jon and move forward, unable to disobey the command. We are deeply enthralled by the power of Ran and her daughters. Their power continues to grow, and I can tell that we are no match for them. Every fiber of my being wants to fight, but the control over my mind is winning, and we march forward.

Jon is pleading with us, "Darla, Mr. Towns, please don't do this. Remember our plan?"

I hear Mother laugh as she says, "They can no longer help you, Bragi. You are now at our mercy."

There is a small rock hallway that leads to an opening up ahead. We march on as instructed until we reach the opening and can see Mother and the cousins gathered in the center around a stone altar, which Jill is strapped to.

Jill has her eyes closed. I can feel that she is still alive but unconscious. There is a cage that holds a giant, snake-like creature behind them, and that is where Mother is leading us. There is also an empty stone throne perched high above, overlooking the altar as if we are expecting royalty to join us.

She commands, "Place Bragi into the cage so he may watch the ceremony, assuming he lasts long enough with the offspring of the Midgard Serpent in there with him."

I know the danger we are putting Jon into, but I cannot stop. Still, I try.

"Mother, please do not make me do this. Place me in there, not Jon."

Mother's command echoes forcefully, "*Bara, do as I command*!"

Dad and I open the cage and throw Jon inside.

He immediately comes running back to the door, begging us, "Darla, please. I love you. Please help me."

The serpent wastes little time. It begins wrapping itself around Jon and pulling him closer and closer.

Then Mother commands, "Now come take your place in our circle, as the ceremony is about to begin."

Dad speaks up, "Ran, have you told our daughters what they are doing?"

Mother snaps, "Of course, they know that we are removing the spell that restricts our movement to and from our realm and that we will soon have the freedom to pass back and forth to wherever we want to go throughout the world."

"Did you tell them what else is about to happen?" Dad asks.

Gaddy speaks up, "We don't care. We want our freedom restored."

"Blodughadda," Dad says, "as bold and bloodthirsty as ever. I am quite sure you don't care about the girl you are about to sacrifice. I am not referring to that, and I'm not referring to the ability to pass through our realm from around the world."

I turn to him. "There is more?"

Dad nods. "I'm afraid so. Now that we are here, if you concentrate, you will know this is true." Dad then tells the story. "When Odin ordered Loki to end our parties and banish us from our realm, Loki made a deal with Ran that she could one day regain her glory, but she had to agree to his terms. Do all of you know what the terms of the deal between the first Ran and Loki are? That's what I want to know."

The daughters of the waves look at each other, but nobody seems to know the answer.

Dad continues, "The deal Loki made requires the sacrifice of a human in order to reverse the spell and also the release of all imprisoned Loki offspring, and I do mean all of them, one at a time. They will rise from wherever they are, and they will also be free to roam the earth and use our portals to pass through and hide out. When we complete this ceremony, there will be all kinds of evil unleashed on the world. This is about much more than the freedom for you girls to move around; it's about the safety of everyone."

Olga speaks up, "That's not true, is it, Mother? Are we also required to release all Loki offspring? Is that really going to happen?"

Mother, sensing that a couple of the girls are wavering, screams, "*Enough*! Aegir, I am tired of you fighting me on this. I cannot tell you how disappointed I am in you and what you have become. You are weak, and you are *not* needed." With that, Mother unleashes a wave of her hand, throwing Dad against the cave wall then against the other side, continuing to slam him back and forth until he is barely conscious.

I shriek in horror, "Mother! No! You are killing him!"

"Exactly," she says, "and you will be next if you fight us, Bara."

Still under their control, I plead with Mother in desperation, "Please, I'll do what you ask, but please stop hurting Dad. I'm begging you. I will never forgive you if you don't stop right now!"

"Do not let me down again, Bara. You won't like what happens if you disobey me."

With that, Dad drops to the ground, alive but barely. He struggles to stay aware and tries to get up but is unable to stand.

We gather around the altar where Jill is and hold hands. As soon as I do, I feel the water again, and I also feel the power surge through me. It's almost an intoxicating feeling. Together, we feel so powerful.

We close our eyes, and one by one, we offer up our powers to the altar, which lights up more and more with each gift.

First, Liv steps forward. Her face is solemn, but there is fire in her eyes. She raises her hands and offers up her power. A shimmering aura surrounds her, and she begins to vanish.

"I offer the power of invisibility," she whispers, and the altar absorbs her gift, glowing brighter as she reappears.

Next is Duff, who steps up with a confident stride. She clears her throat, and her voice echoes eerily around the cavern. "I offer the power to imitate voices." Her voice splits into a dozen different tones, each one distinct and perfect.

The altar drinks in her power, the light intensifying.

Hef steps forward, her movements deliberate and powerful. "I offer the power to make water swell and grow," she declares.

A ripple runs through the water at her feet, and the altar pulses with energy as it takes in her gift.

Ronny follows, her expression calm but focused. "I offer the power to control emotions through water."

A wave of calm washes over me, and the altar glows even brighter as it absorbs her power.

Olga is next, her eyes sharp and determined. "I offer the power to manipulate the wind in water."

The air around us stirs, and the altar's light becomes almost blinding as it takes in the cool breeze of her gift.

Finally, it is my turn. My heart is heavy, and I feel the weight of what we are doing.

"I offer the power to feel what things in the water are feeling," I say, my voice trembling.

The water around us vibrates with emotion, and the altar glows with an intense, almost unbearable light.

Gaddy steps forward last, her expression fierce. "I offer the precious power to kill," she says, her voice cold.

The light from the altar flares violently, and the air is filled with a sense of impending doom.

As we complete this, the power surges in the altar.

Mother then starts reading from an ancient text. "Aegir, Ran, and our nine daughters have gathered in our realm, as required. We are all here and accounted for, as it is written. We call on a descendent of Loki to ascend from the depths below and take his place on the throne we have prepared."

The cavern trembles as her words echo throughout the space. The ground beneath us shakes, and the air becomes heavy with anticipation. The cage where Jon is trapped rattles violently, and the serpent tightens its grip around him.

Jon gasps for breath, his eyes wide with terror. "Darla, please," he whispers, his voice barely audible. "Don't let them do this."

My blood runs cold. This can't be happening.

But before I can react, a figure emerges from the shadows below the altar. We instantly know it is a Loki. My heart skips a beat as I realize this is the same person—being, thing—that kidnapped me at camp this summer. This is not good.

"Ah, Ran," he says, his voice dripping with satisfaction and triumph. "You've done well. The ceremony is almost complete."

Mother's eyes gleam with triumph. "Yes, My Lord. Soon, we will be free to move between realms, and our combined power will be unrivaled."

Loki's grin widens. "Indeed. But there's one more thing to do." He turns to Jill, bound on the altar, and his smile turns sinister. "The sacrifice."

Loki's gaze shifts to Jon, his smile never faltering. "Ah, Jon Bragg. Such passion. Such loyalty. But you're powerless here. Don't you know that you can never defeat me? I am going to keep coming back, over and over, until I end you once and for all. You are going to know and feel the true power I have. When you see your sister die, just know that her death is not going to just free me. It's also going to restore my powers that the APS stripped from me. I will finally be fully back, and I will exact revenge.

"Serpent. squeeze tighter but make sure he watches. Then you may kill him."

I can feel the tears streaming down my face.

Jörmungandr

Jon

THE COLD, DAMP AIR of the cavern hits me like a physical force as I am held in the cage. The iron bars are rough against my skin, and the metallic taste of blood fills my mouth. I watch helplessly as Jill lies on the stone altar, her eyes closed, unaware of the impending doom. Ran and the daughters of the waves stand around her, their expressions filled with a mix of triumph and evil.

Every fiber of my being wants to rush to her, but I'm trapped here, powerless, with a monstrous serpent tightening its grip around me.

The creature, a descendant of the Midgard serpent called Jormungandr, coils itself around my body. Each squeeze forces the air from my lungs, and the world around me starts to blur. As I slip in and out of consciousness, memories and stories flood my mind—tales of the APS hunting down serpents like this one.

The APS has always been vigilant in their quest to maintain balance and order. The descendants of Jormungandr are particularly dangerous, born from the union of Loki and Angrboda, the giantess. These serpents inherited the cunning and malice of their parents, making them formidable adversaries. I recall the stories my grandfather told me about the APS's history with them.

One story, in particular, stands out. It was about a serpent that had taken refuge in the depths of the Amazon River. The APS sent their best agents, including my grandfather, to track and eliminate the creature. The hunt lasted for months, with the serpent using the dense jungle and murky waters to its advantage. The APS had to contend with not just the serpent, but also the hostile environment and the indigenous tribes who worshiped the creature as a god. When they finally cornered it, the battle was fierce and costly. Many lives were lost, but they succeeded in slaying the beast, preventing it from wreaking havoc and producing offspring.

Another story was about a serpent that had hidden in the icy waters of the Arctic. The APS tracked it to a remote glacier, where it had been feeding on the local wildlife and growing stronger. The freezing temperatures and harsh conditions made the hunt a nightmare. The serpent's scales were nearly impervious to their weapons, and its ability to blend with the ice made it almost invisible. After weeks of relentless pursuit, the APS finally managed to trap it in a crevasse and seal it away, ensuring it could never escape.

As I struggle to breathe, the serpent loosens its grip slightly, allowing me just enough air to stay conscious. I can feel its scales, cold and rough against my skin, a constant reminder of my plight. Ran must have been waiting for this moment for a long time, nurturing this serpent in her realm, feeding and caring for it until it was strong enough to serve her.

Ran's voice cuts through my thoughts, her tone dripping with malice. "Bragi, son of Odin, you are now at our mercy. Watch as we restore our power and unleash our wrath upon the world."

At this point, I don't know if she is saying that now or I am just remembering what she said when I was thrown in here. I am confused and disoriented in ways that can only happen from slipping in and out of consciousness.

I can barely keep my eyes open, but I force myself to focus on Jill. She lies there, so still, so vulnerable. I have to do something. I can't let this happen. But the serpent tightens its grip again, and I'm plunged back into darkness.

I remember another of Grandpa's stories. This one was about a serpent that had taken refuge in the deep ocean trenches. The APS had to enlist the help of marine biologists and deep-sea divers to locate it. The serpent had been terrorizing coastal towns, dragging fishermen and their boats into the depths. The APS's mission was fraught with danger, as they had to contend with the crushing pressure of the deep ocean and the serpent's immense size and strength. The final confrontation was a desperate battle, with the APS barely managing to drive the serpent into a dormant underwater volcano, sealing it in there.

These stories, these battles, they all seemed so distant, so far removed from the nightmare I'm living now. But they are a testament to the power of this beast wrapped around me. If only I had my powers, if only I could break free from this cage.

The serpent's grip relaxes again, and I gasp for air, trying to gather my strength.

As this torture continues, I swear that I see the face of Coach Locke looking in at me and enjoying my pain and suffering. I know this cannot be the case because I have already eliminated him several times. And last time, I sent him to Hades. How is it possible that he is back? Or is he? At this point, I cannot be sure. I cannot trust my instincts.

Instincts—what did Mr. Towns say earlier? He said to trust my heart and to watch for a sign.

Is Coach Locke some sort of sign? I doubt it could be any kind of good sign if he is, because he hates me. He's so real, though, and I feel like he is talking to me and to the serpent. The serpent seems to like that and responds to his voice.

I can feel a little tingle emanating from the snake every time I hear Coach Locke's voice. This makes me think that at least the snake is hearing this, too, and it is not just me.

The next gasp of air I take, I see Mr. Towns lying on the floor, clearly in a lot of pain. I reach for him but, of course, that is not possible. Our eyes meet, and I can see he has the look of someone determined to stop something. He has eyes that are almost glowing with rage as he struggles to stand. What is he planning to do? He is definitely outnumbered. I wish I could help.

I try to move, but there is no point, as this serpent is in control.

I feel like the pressure is too much and that I'm not going to be able to endure it any longer. I could crack and explode all over at any point. That reminds me of the eggs that Grandpa used to teach me about protection spells and how to break them. I think about the egg getting smashed in my pocket by Brad and how he wanted to embarrass me. Little did he know that I already learned an important lesson about how Odin works. It's pure love that can compel Odin to release his protection.

However, that was just an egg. What would it take to impact this large of a protection spell? I don't know, but I am going to try.

I'll just repeat whatever I can remember as this ceremony continues. Whatever happens, it cannot be the sacrifice of my sister. There is no way the benevolent Odin would require something so heinous.

I focus on the words being chanted by Ran and the daughters. They're invoking ancient incantations, summoning the power of the realms. Their voices rise and fall in a haunting melody, filling the cavern with a dark, resonant energy. The air around me grows colder, and I can feel the power they're channeling. It's almost suffocating, but I have to stay conscious. I have to find a way to disrupt their ritual.

Just then, Coach Locke orders the snake to release me. The serpent slowly but dutifully follows the order. It seems to take forever, but the pressure is lessening, and I'm starting to become more aware. I'm struck with horror as I realize it *is* Coach Locke. He is standing right before me and not as a draugr, but as human as ever. How is *that* possible? What in the world is going on here?

He smiles and says, "There you are. I want you to take a good look into my eyes so you can see who is doing this to your sister. As soon as this sacrifice is complete, all of my ancestors and descendants will be released from every realm. The beauty of all of this is we will have your family to thank. Oh, this is such poetic justice." He lets out a loud and thunderous roar of laughter.

I look to Jill then back to Coach Locke, and then I put my head down and close my eyes. I cannot watch this. I will not watch this happen.

"Open your eyes!" he demands. "Open your eyes, or I will let the serpent kill you now!"

I raise my head and say a little prayer for my sister. I love her so much. Then I look over at Darla with tears starting to stream down my face, and I see she is crying, as well. It's almost too much to withstand.

Then Ran says, "With this sacrifice, we fulfill our obligation to Loki, and we collect our reward." She raises a large sword above Jill, and I close my eyes as she starts to lower it.

I hear Darla scream. "Nooooooooooo!"

Sacrifice

Darla

THE CAVERN IS FILLED with an oppressive silence, only broken by the heavy breaths of the gathered figures and the distant roars of beasts below.

Just as Mother raises her sword, preparing to bring it down on Jill, Dad breaks through the circle, throwing himself over Jill to shield her with his body. In a split-second, he looks up at me, his eyes full of love and determination, and declares, "Love you, darlin.'"

Mother's sword pierces through Dad, and the ground trembles violently.

The screams of anger from the evil beings below echo throughout the cavern. The altar begins to shake as the beings below pound against it in chaotic, uncontrollable waves, trying to break through. Something is wrong. Terribly wrong.

I scream, but the sound is drowned out by the roar of the cavern and the turmoil within me. My heart shatters as I run to Dad, cradling his lifeless body in my arms.

"Mother, how could you? You killed him. You killed Dad!" I sob, my tears falling freely.

Even Mother seems rattled by what happened.

"Oh no, no, no, no! What did you do, Aegir?" Mother screams, her voice tinged with panic.

"What did *he* do? What did *you* do, Mother?" I retort, my voice breaking with grief and anger.

"No, he ruined everything. We have spent years planning this, all for this moment, and he *ruined* it! That was our one chance! All he had to do was just lie there, and everything would have been perfect. But he couldn't even manage that! He's such a disappointment to this family!"

"No, Mother, it's *you*! You did this, and I am done with you!" I yell, my rage boiling over. Then I pick up the sword she used to slay Dad, and with all the fury and hatred I feel, I plunge it into her.

She staggers forward, grasping at the sword lodged in her body. "That's my girl," she gasps. "You finally are acting like the giant you are!"

"No, Mother! You do not get to take joy in this, because you are evil. You were willing to kill this innocent girl all to gain some stupid power. Were we not enough? Why weren't Dad and I enough for you? Why did you have to have more?"

She looks straight at me, her breath ragged. "That's what giants do, my dear. That's what giants do," she repeats with her last breath before collapsing to the ground.

The ground shifts again, the altar continuing to shake, and the beasts below roar even louder.

Loki's voice cuts through the chaos. "No! This was not the deal. You were supposed to sacrifice a human, not each other! You stupid girls! You have ruined everything!"

Gaddy and the cousins gather around, showing mixed emotions. Olga runs to comfort me, while Gaddy and Ronny rush to Mother, checking her pulse before letting her drop back down.

Gaddy glares at me, fury in her eyes. "She's gone. You have wrecked this for all of us!"

Loki looks at Gaddy and says, "Well, technically, you are all still here. You aren't all breathing, but you are all still here. Shall we try this again?"

I glance over at Jon, his face pale and desperate as he struggles in the serpent's renewed grip. I know I have to act quickly.

I run to the altar and untie Jill, who is still unconscious but breathing. "Stay with me, Jill," I whisper, trying to shake her awake.

Jon's eyes meet mine, filled with a mix of hope and fear. "Darla, we need to end this. We need to stop them."

Loki's cold laughter fills the cavern. "*End this*? Oh, Bragi, you have no idea what you're up against. Your father's protection spell may have stripped your powers, but it hasn't stripped theirs. This is just a minor setback."

Gaddy, still fuming, turns to Loki. "What do you mean? How do we continue?"

Loki smirks, his eyes gleaming with malice. "There are always options, my dear Blodughadda. Sacrificing a human is but one way to break the spell. There are other rituals, other deals that can be made. But they come with a price."

"What price?" Gaddy asks, her voice defiant.

Loki's smile widens. "A life for a life. A soul for a soul. If you wish to complete the ceremony and gain the freedom you so desire, one of you must willingly offer yourself as a replacement. The sacrifice must be willing, and the offering must be pure."

The cousins exchange uneasy glances. The weight of Loki's words hang heavy in the air.

"And what happens if we don't?" I ask, my voice barely above a whisper.

Loki's expression darkens. "Then you will remain trapped in this realm, powerless and defeated. The portal will close, and you will never have the freedom you seek."

I look at Jill, still unconscious but alive, and then at Jon, who is fighting to stay conscious. My heart aches with the enormity of the decision before me.

"There has to be another way," I say, desperation creeping into my voice.

Loki chuckles. "There is no other way, Bara. You must choose. Will you sacrifice your own freedom for the sake of others? Or will you condemn all of us to eternal captivity?"

Dad's voice echoes in my mind, his final words to me. "Love you, darlin'." I know what he would want me to do. He gave his life to protect Jill, to stop this madness. I can't let his sacrifice be in vain.

"I'll do it." I step forward. "I'll be the sacrifice. But you have to promise that Jill and Jon will go free and be returned back to the beach safely."

"No, Darla!" Jon shouts, his voice hoarse with desperation and from the pressure of the serpent.

I turn to him, my heart breaking at the sight of his anguish. "It's the only way, Jon. I have to end this. I have to help them."

Loki's grin widens. "Excellent. The willing sacrifice of a giantess, the daughter of Aegir and Ran, will be more than sufficient. I agree to your terms, girlie, especially since that Bragi will suffer knowing that he lives because you died."

Olga's eyes flash with anger. "No, we can't let her do this! There has to be another way!"

"There isn't," Loki says coldly. "This is the only way to complete the ceremony and gain your freedom."

I take a deep breath, steeling myself for what is to come. "What do I need to do?"

Loki's eyes gleam with satisfaction. "Kneel before the altar and place your hands upon it. The power you have given will return to you, and you will be consumed by it. Your sacrifice will complete the ritual and open the portal."

I move toward the altar, my heart pounding in my chest. The power I felt earlier surges within me, a wild, uncontrollable force. I kneel before the altar, placing my hands on its cold, hard surface.

The energy pulses through me, growing stronger with each passing moment.

Loki begins to chant, his voice low and resonant. The ground shakes beneath me, and the air crackles with electricity. I can feel the power building, threatening to tear me apart.

Jon's voice breaks through the haze of power and pain. "Darla, please!" However, the serpent is choking the life out of him.

I look at him, tears streaming down my face. "I love you, Jon. Take care of Jill. Take care of each other."

Before Jon can respond, Loki's chant reaches its climax, and power surges through me, overwhelming my senses. I feel myself being lifted from the ground, the energy consuming me.

The cavern is filled with a blinding light, the power of the ritual reaching its peak. The ground shakes violently, and the portal begins to open. The daughters of the waves stand around the altar, their expressions a mix of anticipation and fear.

Loki's laughter echoes through the cavern. "The portal is opening!"

But as the light begins to fade, something unexpected happens. The power that has consumed me doesn't dissipate. Instead, it returns to the altar, pulsing with a strange, unfamiliar energy.

"What's happening?" Gaddy shouts, her voice filled with panic.

Loki's eyes widen in shock. "This isn't right! The power should have been absorbed!"

The altar begins to crack, the energy within it growing unstable. The ground beneath us starts to give way, and the cavern walls tremble.

"What have we done?" Olga's voice trembles with fear.

The portal flickers, its edges fraying and unstable. The beasts below roar in anger, their fury shaking the foundation of the cavern.

Loki's expression twists with rage. "You fools! You've ruined everything!"

As the cavern continues to collapse, I feel a strange calm wash over me. I have done what I could to stop them, to save Jon and Jill. My sacrifice has not been in vain.

The last thing I hear is Loki's furious scream, and then I fall to the ground, the wind knocked out of me for a brief moment.

The Light

Jon

AS I STRUGGLE FOR AIR, the giant serpent seizes its opportunity to end me.

I just witnessed the most honorable sacrifice I have ever seen from Mr. Towns and the most terrifying thing as I saw Darla attack her mother. My heart is ripping apart for her as I realize that she has lost both of her parents, and it seems as though she is going to lose me, too.

Then it gets even worse.

I can no longer talk, or I would scream at the top of my lungs not to trust Coach Locke, a Loki. You can never deal with him. It can only end in a fate far worse than you could possibly imagine. Yet, the cousins and Darla agreed to make a deal—to sacrifice Darla in order to gain favor with the gods and complete the ceremony.

As I slip into a sleep from the lack of oxygen, I remember what Darla's father said again—trust your heart, and you will know when it is time.

I just witnessed the purest form of unconditional love in the sacrifice that her dad made and, in the sacrifice, she is now willing to make one to save Jill and possibly me if this serpent doesn't end me right now.

I see an extremely bright light and I don't know if this is the end and the light that so many people say they see before death or if this is actually happening. I force my eyes open in tiny slits so that I can see what is happening.

I see Darla hovering above all of us as power completely takes control over her. She is like a beautiful angel above me, and she looks so stunning. I love her so much I can barely stand it.

Suddenly, I hear Grandpa's voice, reminding me of what it takes to break the protection spell of Odin. It takes an act of selfless love and sacrifice. Surely, what I just witnessed would qualify for that.

If Odin is truly fair, then he should listen to my words. So, I start to whisper, as that is all my voice cand do right now.

"Odin, father of Bragi,
I request you lift your spell.
A man has given his life,
A life that he lived so well.
His sacrifice was so pure,
Do not let it be done in vain.
End your protection now,
So I can stop all this pain."

With that, the power shoots from Darla and back into the altar, slamming the door shut against those who were trying to cross into our realm. I waste no time as I can feel my powers returning. I need to be free of this monster.

I decide to communicate with the beast that is strangling me.

"Oh, serpent from the past,
You no longer need to fight.
Release me from your grip,
So I can be free tonight."

The serpent obeys and releases me.

I then turn my attention to the cage that is holding me. However, before I can utter a rhyme, the cage collapses from the shifting ground, and I jump under the beast that was choking me so he absorbs the blow. I feel the last breath from the serpent and make my way to my feet, to see Coach Locke standing before me. He is angry and I prepare for a fight.

"Bragi, I want to end you so badly, but I have no power to match yours. You now have a choice. This realm is collapsing around us. You can either end me or you can save your sister, your girlie, and yourself. There isn't time to do both, so what will it be?"

I struggle for a moment, trying to decide what the right thing to do is right now. If I don't deal with him, he may find his way out of here and harm others. If I deal with him and don't save Jill and Darla, then all of what has happened here would be for nothing.

Decision made, I turned from Coach Locke to find Jill. I see Coach Locke running with the cousins out of the corner of my eye. Jill is still unconscious and unable to walk, and Darla is trying her best but cannot take Jill out of here on her own. Her cousins are all fleeing for the archway and the exit from this realm.

I run over to Darla and ask, "What do you think we should do? What's the best way to get Jill out of here?"

"Can you carry her?" Darla asks.

"I think I can."

I pick up my sister, holding her in my arms as we run as quickly as we can through the hallway, through the archway, back through the maze, and then we reach the exit to the water. To our surprise, Olga is there still, waiting for us.

"Darla, we can take them back together."

Darla questions, "Are you sure? Dad and I could only bring one into the realm."

She answers, "I'm sure. We can take Jill. Jon can use his magic."

I almost forgot that's an option, which makes no sense because I literally just used my powers to break the spell.

I nod, and Olga and Darla take Jill. Then I turn to look back at Coach Locke, but he is nowhere to be seen.

"I will take my leave from this place,

and land back up on the lake shore.

I call on the gods to seal this realm,

So no one can enter or leave anymore."

I step through the portal and, as I do, I turn to see the opening vanish. Then I am pulled rapidly through the water until I reach the shore.

When I arrive, I see that Olga, Darla, and Jill are already there.

Darla comes running to me and leaps into my arms, knocking me over and back into the water. We stand back up, I shrug, and she places her head on my shoulder, tightening her hold on me as she breaks down sobbing. I hold her tightly, knowing that nothing I say will stop the pain she is feeling. I just need to be here for her.

The chaos we just escaped was overwhelming. The cavern, with its cold, damp air and oppressive atmosphere, is now behind us. But the memories of what happened there are seared into my brain. I can still hear the echo of Darla's scream, the sound of the ground shaking, and the roars of the beasts below. The image of her father's sacrifice plays over and over in my head, a testament to his love and bravery.

The moonlight reflects off the lake, casting an eerie glow on everything. The water is calm now, a stark contrast to the turmoil beneath its surface. It's hard to believe that, just moments ago, we were fighting for our lives in a place filled with ancient beasts and malevolent giants. The serene lake feels like a cruel joke, masking the horrors that lie just below its surface.

I look at Jill, still unconscious but breathing steadily. Her face is pale, and she has a few scratches and bruises, but she is alive. I silently says a prayer, grateful for her being safe.

The realization that we made it out, that we are alive, begins to sink in. But the cost was high. Darla lost her father and, in a way, her mother, too, though she never truly had her to begin with.

I glance over at Olga, who is standing a little apart, her face a mixture of relief and sorrow. She stayed to help us, risking her own safety. There is more to her than I initially thought. Her loyalty to Darla is evident, but so is her compassion. Without her, Jill wouldn't have made it out.

Darla's sobs eventually subside into quiet tears. She pulls back slightly, looking into my eyes. Her face is streaked with tears, and her eyes are red, but there is strength there, too.

"Jon, thank you," she whispers, her voice trembling.

I shake my head. "You don't need to thank me. We all did this together. Your dad ... he was incredible. He saved us. *You* saved us."

She nods, her expression a mixture of grief and determination. "He always said he would do anything to protect us. I just ... I never thought it would come to this."

I don't know what to say. No words can make this better. So, I just hold her hand, letting her know I am here.

Olga walks over, her eyes scanning the horizon. "We should move. We don't know if any of the others will come after us. We need to find a safe place to regroup."

I agree. "We need to get Jill to a hospital, or to the APS. We don't know what they may have done to her or what long-term effects it could have, if any."

Olga says, "We used some natural herbs to subdue her. I'm sorry, but I helped. I can tell them exactly what we did. Although, it should wear off on its own, and she should be fine."

As we pick up Jill to get her medical care, we see a bunch of vehicles in the distance, heading our way.

The Rescue

Darla

WE SEARCH FOR THE TAHOE to leave because we know we need the room to lay Jill down, but it's clear that the other cousins took it. I then look around frantically for the Corolla.

"Jon, where is your car?" I ask, panic making me raise my voice.

"Shoot, Marc took it to go get Grandpa," Jon replies, his face pale with worry.

"Why would he get your grandpa and not your parents?"

"Because Grandpa is Bragi, like me, and he works with the APS. Well, he's retired now, but he worked for them his whole career."

"Those are the people who came to the camp this summer, right?" I remember the official-looking people who descended upon the camp, their presence erasing the memories of those who had witnessed what happened and told them that I had run off and gotten lost.

"Yep, they help clean up scenes and make sure that the local police and news organizations don't get involved."

"How exactly do they do that?" I know what they did to Jenny and me; I just want to be sure.

"Well, you know, they come in and make sure that any survivors forget what they have seen so they cannot tell the world about us."

"How are they going to do that this time? Everyone left."

"Well, there wasn't much that anyone saw because everyone was knocked out and barely caught a glimpse of Jill getting carried away.

That is relatively easily explained. When Jill shows up, that should be enough to make them move on."

"What about you? What are you going to say? Are you going to tell them what I did?" My voice wavers as I contemplate the potential consequences.

"I'm only going to tell them what they need to know, Darla. You can trust me, and Olga, as well. Right, Olga?" Jon turns to Olga, who nods in agreement.

As soon as Jon finishes speaking, a long line of vehicles arrive. They don't have sirens on, but it's clear they are officials of some kind.

As they pull up, we look at each other, and Jon says, "They're here."

When the cars stop beside us, Marc and Jon's grandpa are the first on the scene, pulling up in the Corolla. Marc comes running over to Jon, and Grandpa heads straight for Jill.

Jon quickly explains to his grandpa, "We tried to leave, but we didn't have a good way to move Jill. Marc had my car, and Darla's cousins took hers. We were stranded."

Jon's grandpa, with a grave expression, says, "It's fine, Jon. The APS has a medical team that will take care of Jill."

The APS's emergency response team, including paramedics, rush to check on Jill. They put her on a stretcher and take her back to their vehicle, rattling off her vital signs. I'm not able to understand what they are saying, but I cling to the hope in their voices.

As they take her back to their ambulance, they pause by Jon's grandpa to say, "She'll be fine. She is just sedated. She will likely wake up from this with no recollection of what happened."

The same lady who approached everyone at the camp comes over and says, "Well, it looks like we meet again here at Harmony Grove. We have to find a better way next time. Did you get lost again, Darla?"

"No, ma'am, I didn't. I didn't get lost last time, either. You and I both know what really happened."

She takes a look back at the men who are with her and asks, "You remember?"

"Yes, ma'am. I remember everything that happened this summer."

She looks surprised. "How is that possible?"

"Because, ma'am, you are aware of the story of Aegir, Ran, and the nine daughters of the waves, right?"

"Yes, we are aware of the gods of the sea and their daughters."

"I am a descendant of Bara. My cousin, Olga, is a descendant of Kolga, and the rest of the nine daughters left in our Tahoe tonight."

She seems taken aback. "I see. Well, where are Aegir and Ran?"

"Those are my parents, ma'am, and they ... they didn't make it." My voice breaks as I explain the fate of my parents.

I proceed to describe everything that happened tonight to the APS. They listen carefully as I describe everyone falling asleep as we briefly saw Jill getting taken, how we found and freed my father, who was bound at the bottom of the lake, and our journey into our underground realm. I break down again as I recount how Dad was beaten then sacrificed himself to save Jill. Reluctantly, I then describe how I killed Mother and the deal we made with Loki. Finally, I detail how it ended and how we brought Jill back to safety.

The APS lady asks, "Is that everything, Darla?"

"Yes, ma'am, that's everything," I reply, my voice trembling with exhaustion and fear of punishment.

Sam comes limping over to us. I run to give him a hug, but he grimaces in pain, so I then help him walk him over to the APS lady.

"Sam, what happened to you?" Jon asks.

"I heard a commotion, and I came running back toward the beach from where I was waiting. I saw your cousins rise out of the water. Two of them were helping a man to shore. I approached him to see who or what he was and to assess the threat level. As I came closer to question him, he charged me and stabbed me with a sword. I was shocked when it happened, as nothing has pierced my skin like that before. I tried to chase after him into the woods, but he got away. Then I came back here."

The lady asks, "Young man, are you also aware of who we are and what we do?"

"Yes, ma'am, I am aware, and I should tell you that I'm a skinwalker."

The lady looks at Jon's grandpa and asks, "How many more surprises are there here in Grinwell?"

Jon steps in, "Just Sam, Darla, and the rest of the nine daughters of the waves. I doubt we will be seeing them any time soon, though, and it sounds like Sam ran into Loki."

The lady asks, "Where are the rest of the girls?"

"I suppose they are back at the farm," I answer.

Looking at Jon, Marc, and Jon's grandpa, she says, "You three, go with the ambulance and take care of the girl, and take the skinwalker with you. We are going to want to bring him in for questioning, but get him medical attention first. Make sure they know it was a magical sword in case they need to do something before he heals on his own." She then turns to Olga and me. "You two, come with us. Let's see if we can find the rest of your siblings."

We drive out to the farm, but nobody is there. All of their rooms are in disarray, as they clearly quickly packed and left. I assume they went back to wherever they came from.

The APS come into our house and start investigating. They take computers and any papers that they can find. They want to do whatever they can to find the remaining daughters of the waves.

After that, they take Olga and me back to their offices since we are minors and they need to decide what to do with us.

As we drive to the APS headquarters, I can't help but feel a profound sense of loss. The drive is long and silent, punctuated only by the occasional whispers between Olga and the APS lady.

The weight of the night's events press heavily on my chest. The thought of facing the future without my dad is almost unbearable.

At the headquarters, the APS officials treat us kindly but with an air of detachment. They are professionals, after all, accustomed to dealing with supernatural crises. We are ushered into a room with soft lighting and comfortable chairs. It feels oddly calming, but my nerves are frayed and I can't relax.

The APS lady, whose name I learn is Agent Collins, sits across from us, her expression compassionate yet firm. "Darla, Olga, we are going to take care of you. We just need to understand your situations a bit better. Darla, do you have any other relatives we can contact?"

I shake my head, tears welling up in my eyes again. "No, ma'am. My parents are gone, and I don't know where the rest of my family is. I'm all alone."

Agent Collins nods sympathetically. "I understand. We'll figure something out."

She then turns to Olga. "What about you? Do you have family nearby?"

Olga nods. "No, ma'am, not nearby. I have family in Bergen, Norway, where we're from. They will be expecting me to come home."

Agent Collins makes a note of this. "All right. We'll arrange for you to be reunited with your family.

"As for you, Darla, we'll find a safe place for you. You're not alone in this. It took a lot of courage to do what you did, and we thank you."

I appreciate her words, but they do little to ease the ache in my heart. The enormity of what happened—the loss of my father, the betrayal and death of my mother, and the weight of all of our actions—weighs heavily on my soul.

I glance at Olga, who seems more composed, though I know she is just as shaken as I am.

"Thank you, Agent Collins," I manage to say, my voice barely above a whisper.

She gives me a reassuring smile. "You're welcome, Darla. We're here to help you. Now, get some rest. We'll start sorting things out in the morning."

As Olga and I are led to a small room with two beds, I can't help but feel the overwhelming exhaustion take over. The bed feels like a haven, and as soon as my head hits the pillow, I am out.

My dreams are a tumultuous mix of memories and nightmares, but through it all, I feel a glimmer of hope. Despite the darkness, there is still a chance for light. I just really want to stay in Grinwell. I need to be near him. I need to be near Jon.

The Letter

Jon

THE AMBULANCE TAKES us to a medical facility specifically set up for the APS. They determine that Jill is miraculously fine once the sedative wears off, which only takes a couple of hours. After that, she is visited by a nurse who explains what happened to her.

"Hello, Jill. You had quite the scare tonight, didn't you? You have to be more careful when swimming in the lake. It gets really deep, and the current can be strong at times. Next time, make sure you stay within the safe swimming area and don't wander off beyond the safety markers. You were really lucky, weren't you?"

Jill says, "Yes, I was really lucky. Thank you, ma'am."

Sam, Grandpa, Marc, and I are filled in on what to say if anyone asks about the situation, and then each of us take turns being questioned. Since I know Darla already told the truth, I am able to be as detailed as possible. It does feel good to not have to hold anything back.

They ask me how long I have known that Darla is one of the daughters of the waves. I admit that I have known something is different about her because she remembered what happened at camp. However, I could honestly say that she just told me what she is earlier in the day.

They are interested in the sword that was used to kill Aegir and Ran. I tell them that we left as quickly as possible, as the realm became unstable. However, I assume that is what Loki used to harm

Sam. It was a part of the ritual, so no doubt it was imbued with magic of some sort. It would take something like that to penetrate the skin of a skinwalker.

They ask me about Sam, and I remind them that is why we sent DNA samples to them, as we suspected he was a skinwalker but needed to prove it. We didn't want to cause unnecessary disruptions by naming names until we were sure it was him. We wouldn't have kept the information from the APS once we confirmed his identity. I know what my responsibility is to report and register other people with powers.

The APS seem satisfied with those responses, and after a couple of hours and making sure Jill is well-hydrated, we are released.

When we get home, after dropping Marc off, Mom and Dad are waiting for us. They are not happy with how late it is and scold both Jill and I for not texting them. When they find out that Jill was saved after wandering out in the lake though, they quickly switch over to concern and appreciation for Jill and I being home safe and sound.

Mom says, "This doesn't excuse you from communicating with us. Next time something like this happens, you be sure to let us know immediately. It's good that you got Grandpa, but you need to let *us* know, Jon. We want to be there to help."

She then turns to Grandpa. "Dad, thank you, but next time, come and get us. Don't leave us in the dark when one of our kids is at risk."

Grandpa just nods and says, "I'm sorry. I was so concerned about helping Jill that I forgot to be reasonable. Please, forgive me."

Dad grabs Jill, Mom, and I in an embrace, and Mom waves in Grandpa.

"All that matters is our family is safe and sound, and together," Dad says. "We love you all so much, but don't scare us like that ever again. Agreed?"

We all say, "Agreed."

Mom then says, "Now, let's get you off to bed. We can talk more about this in the morning."

Mom walks Jill up to her room to tuck her in and care for her as only she can do, and Grandpa walks to my room with me.

He asks, "I know you are tired, but can you tell me more about what happened tonight?"

I nod. "Of course, Grandpa."

I explain to him that I lost my powers when they took Jill, and, somehow, they managed to put everyone to sleep, including Darla. It was Sam who woke Darla, and then Darla woke me. If it wasn't for Sam, I'm not sure how much longer we would have been out.

Since I couldn't use my powers, we were stuck in a dangerous position, and we had to rely on Darla to find her dad, and then we had to rely on him to lead us to where we needed to go. I then describe what it felt like to be carried into their realm and what I saw when I got down there.

I then describe how Darla's mother had a cage down there that held a descendant of Jörmungandr. I can barely describe for him the feeling of the beast wrapped around me as I struggled to breathe between the pulsating rounds of pressure against my chest and neck. It was terrifying, and I never wished for my powers more than right at that moment.

I explain how Coach Locke appeared—at least, what I could remember of it. Most importantly, it was him, and he was fully human somehow. Whatever deal Ran had with Loki must have been powerful to bring him back from Hades. Honestly, I can't even believe that happened.

Grandpa has already heard the rest, so we don't need to continue, but he says, "Jon, we have to be careful, as we can assume that Coach Locke is going to come for you again."

"I know."

"That means that we are going to need to be extra diligent and on high alert."

Once again, I tell him, "I know."

Grandpa nods. "That's enough for tonight, Jon. If you think of anything else, we can talk about it tomorrow. Goodnight."

"Goodnight, Grandpa. Love you."

"Love you, too, Jon. I'm glad you are safe."

As I slip into bed, my thoughts immediately drift to Darla. I wonder where she is tonight. Is she okay? She just experienced something that no child should ever have to go through. She watched her mother kill her father, and then, in anger and desperation to stop her, she killed her own mother. That's overwhelming for anyone, and I can only imagine how she must feel.

I know her mother and her never really got along, but I can't imagine finding out that one of your parents is so power-hungry that they would willingly sacrifice one of your friends to gain power. Then, in doing that, kill the other parent. In spite of all of that, she is going to mourn the loss of her mother, too. Family is family, and it cannot ever be forgotten.

As I gradually fall to sleep, the night starts off rough, with nightmares. Then I get a visit from Sam in wolf form. He thanks me for helping to take care of Darla and Jill, saying it was brave to go to their realm, knowing that I had no powers and could be walking into a trap. He then approaches me and, with a nudge of his nose against my head, says, "Rest."

I fall asleep, and for the rest of the night, I am not bothered by anything.

THE REST OF THE WEEKEND is a somber one, as I haven't heard from Darla. I don't know where she is or what might be happening to her. She's all I can think about.

I ask Grandpa, but he doesn't have any updates, either. It's the longest weekend of my life, mostly because of the unknown. I then decide to write a letter to her and ask Grandpa to get it to her at the APS.

Darla,

I wanted to let you know how much my heart hurts for you right now. I know you have been through more than anyone should ever have to endure. This summer, it was all my fault, and I still feel horrible about that, but that pales in comparison to what you had to go through this weekend.

I want you to know that my love for you is real. I cannot thank you enough for helping Jill and for being so willing to sacrifice everything for her and for me. You are a true hero, and your heart is bigger than I deserve to hold, but I want to hold it.

Whenever you are ready—there's no rush—I'll go with you back to Harmony Grove to pay our respects to your parents. It may take time for you to want to do that, but if you don't mind, I would love to be there for you.

I don't know where you are going to end up, and I don't know how, but I will find you and be there for you for as long as you will have me. There is no doubt in my mind that it's only you for me, and you can count on me forever. I love you, darlin'.

Together forever

- Jon

Homecoming

Darla

IT'S BEEN SEVERAL DAYS since the incident at the lake. I've really lost track while staying here, at the APS headquarters. I'm not being held against my will; I just don't have any other place to go. I know that word has gotten out that my parents were killed in a freak accident at the farm and my "cousins" have been sent back to where they are from. Well, at least, that is the story the APS created and fed to the local authorities and the news.

In reality, the APS turned the gas stove on, spewing gas throughout the farmhouse, and then lit a match as they walked out of the front door, as if it was nothing. They were kind enough to allow me to grab some things from my room and some of my dad's belongings. I just need something to remember him by—the watch that he said was passed down for generations to him, his favorite pocketknife, and a couple of his T-shirts. They are super big, but sleeping in them helps me get some rest. I don't need or want anything from Mother. I may regret that someday, but right now, I just can't go there.

I will miss my dad every day for the rest of my life. There is literally nobody who could ever replace him. He was a kind, gentle soul who was always there for me, offering words of wisdom, protecting me and inspiring me to be the best person I can be, all while keeping me sane when the world around me seemed like too much.

I have been talking to the APS psychologist every day, and it's not really getting any better. There is no doubt that part of me also died that night. The innocence in me is lost forever, as I have to live with the fact that my mother killed my father, and I killed her. I could sugarcoat it by saying that I did the world a favor, but I know in my heart that it was blind rage that caused me to attack her, and that scares me a little. Maybe she is right; maybe I am her daughter and that killing is just a part of my DNA. I don't want to be a monster. I want to be a good person, a good giant, like Dad.

Right now, I need to find a way to move on with my life. I want to seek closure, but I'm not sure how to do that. The doctor keeps telling me that I'll find a way when I am ready, but that sounds like a crock to me. All I hear when someone says that is that I'm on my own.

The APS is going to sell the farm and put that money in a trust for me. I won't be able to access it until I am eighteen. Still, they offer to send me anywhere in the world that I want to go. However, the only place I want to be is back at Grinwell-Bluehill High with my friends—Sam, Taylor, Jenny, Jess and, of course, Jon. I miss all of them so much.

Now I need to decide who I can ask to see if I can stay with them. If I don't figure that out soon, I'm sure they will take matters into their own hands.

Jenny's family would be great, but I already know they can barely make ends meet as it is, and one more mouth to feed won't help. The only person I am close to who has more money than they know what to do with is Jess. It seems like she is my best option. Her family has known my family for years because of our dance company, and they clearly have the means. In fact, their home is so nice that it could be on the cover of *Better Homes & Gardens*. I don't know if they would be willing, but I have to just go for it.

I take the phone from Agent Collins and call Jess. "Hello, Jess?"

She screams, "Darla! Are you okay? I'm so sorry to hear about your parents. We are all worried sick. Where are you?"

"I have been staying with Child Protective Services since the explosion at the farm."

"Where is that?" she asks.

"Close by, but not close enough to go to school."

"Darla, we all miss you so much! Is there anything we can do to help?"

"Well, that's sort of why I am calling, Jess. I really want to come back to Grinwell, but I don't have anyone to stay with who could be my guardian. I am kind of embarrassed to ask, and you can say no if you want, but do you think you could ask your parents if I could come and live with you?"

Jess screams a joyous, "Yes, yes, Darla! I'll go ask them right now." She's so excited that she drops her phone, and I hear her walking out of the room. Then I hear excited murmurs back and forth for what seems like forever. She finally comes back to the phone, "Darla?"

"Yes?"

"Sorry about the delay. I wanted to fill Mom in on everything. She's right here and wants to talk to whoever is in charge over there."

I hand the phone back to Agent Collins, who explains, "Darla needs a legal guardian and, unfortunately, she has no known living relatives of age. Would you be willing to take her in so she can finish high school?" The agent nods and looks over to me with a smile. "Great. We will need to run some background checks and get the paperwork together. Do you think we could meet at your place for a home visit tomorrow?" She nods again then ends the call with, "Perfect. We'll see you then."

Agent Collins then tells me, "We will run some quick checks just to be sure, and this is only temporary, but you can go and live with them as long as there are no red flags in the system."

"Perfect. Thank you, Agent Collins."

When we arrived at Jess's house the next day, it's even more beautiful than I thought. In fact, it's amazing. The front of the house boasts a beautifully landscaped garden with a stone pathway leading to a grand double-door entrance. The exterior is painted a soft cream color, with large windows that allow natural light to flood in. As we walk up to the doors, I notice the intricate woodwork around the entrance, giving it a timeless elegance.

Jess's mother greets us warmly and invites us inside. The interior is equally stunning. The foyer opens up to a spacious living room with high ceilings and large, comfortable sofas arranged around a stone fireplace. The walls are adorned with tasteful artwork, and the hardwood floors shine with a polished finish. It has five bedrooms, and she says that every bedroom has an attached bathroom. This has virtually nothing in common with our old farmhouse.

Jess's mother leads me upstairs to my new room.

The guest room—my room for now—is a cozy yet elegant space. The walls are painted a soft lavender, and there's a large window with a view of the backyard pool. The bed is covered with a fluffy, white comforter, and there's a matching set of bedside tables with vintage lamps. A desk sits in one corner, perfect for studying, and a plush armchair is positioned near the window for reading. Jess has moved some of her dance trophies into my room, making it feel more like home since I had several of the same trophies in my old room. Almost everything was destroyed in the fire, so having these little touches means the world to me.

Jess's mother asks, "Do you have enough clothes, dear?"

I shake my head, feeling a bit embarrassed. "I only have a few things that a fireman rushed in and grabbed for me. Almost everything was lost in the fire."

Jess takes my hand and leads me to her closet. "Grab whatever you need," she says with a smile.

Her closet is enormous, filled with all kinds of clothes, from casual wear to formal dresses. I go ahead and pick out a few simple items, grateful for her generosity.

The next day, after getting ready for school, we are called down to eat breakfast together. Jess's mom has prepared a feast: pancakes, eggs, bacon, and fresh fruit. I do my best to thank Jess's mom and dad for taking me in and tell them I will try not to be too much of a bother. They reassure me that they are just glad they can help and that I am welcome to stay as long as I need. I can tell they mean it and are not just saying that.

When we arrive at school, I feel a mix of anxiety and excitement as we pull up in her pink sports car that everyone instantly recognizes. The reception is a bit too much for me, but I'm never going to let on or complain.

As I turn the corner to go to my locker, I see Jon. Even after several days, he is there, waiting for me, hoping I will show up. I have no doubt that this is part of his daily routine.

As soon as he sees me, his eyes light up, and I can't contain myself. I run over to him and give him a huge hug. Of course, that leads to a bunch of whistling and comments from the other kids, but I don't care. I am here, I am with Jon, and I am home.

I start to talk. "I got your letter."

Jon starts talking, as well. "I missed you so much. Wait—you got my letter?"

"I missed you, too, Jon, and yes, I got your letter. Thank you. I'm sorry I couldn't write back."

"Darla, I was so worried that I wasn't going to see you again."

"I'm right here, Jon."

He gets down on one knee. "Darla Towns, I have one question to ask you in front of all these people."

Now, literally everyone is watching us.

"Um, what, Jon?"

"Darla, would you ...?" Jon pauses for what seems like forever, and I am starting to get a little anxious about what could be coming next. "Would you go to the homecoming dance with me?"

I pause in a moment of relief then smile. "Of course, Jon, I would love to go to homecoming with you!"

That brings applause from all of the students surrounding us, and Jon stands up to give me a hug.

"That's awesome, Darla, awesome!"

I lean into him and whisper in his ear, "You can call me *darlin'.*"

Don't miss out!

Visit the website below and you can sign up to receive emails whenever Kenney Myers publishes a new book. There's no charge and no obligation.

https://books2read.com/r/B-A-KKJN-NZZQD

BOOKS 2 READ

Connecting independent readers to independent writers.

Also by Kenney Myers

Jon Bragg
Jon Bragg Blue Essence
Jon Bragg Scout's Honor
Jon Bragg Giant Problem

Watch for more at https://www.kenneymyers.com.

About the Author

Kenney Myers is a husband and father of three children living and working in the Houston, TX area. He is originally from a small town in Iowa where he and his wife Jolene were high school sweethearts.

He received his bachelor's degree from Grand View University and his master's degree from Upper Iowa University, both also in the Hawkeye state.

You may be familiar with him as an actor in various films and TV shows or as a technology entrepreneur. He is best known for the TV show Kindly Kenney which is distributed worldwide by UKW Media and for appearing in dozens of holiday movies. You can follow his acting career on IMDB.

Kenney enjoys writing fiction and creating worlds where characters develop and master special abilities. It's a great escape for him as a writer and is consistent with the types of books he loves to read.

Read more at https://www.kenneymyers.com.

Printed in the USA
CPSIA information can be obtained
at www.ICGtesting.com
JSHW022128190724
66691JS00005B/128